MY TRUTH
MY TIME
MY TURN

My Son's Wife Series

Get more Info About Shelia E. Bell books!

Additional titles by Shelia E. Bell
(Some titles can be found under former name Shelia Lipsey)

<u>*Young Adult Titles*</u>
House of Cars
The Life of Payne
The Lollipop Girl
The Righteous Brothers (Coming 2019)

<u>*Standalone Novels*</u>
Show A Little Love (*out of print*)
Always Now and Forever Love Hurts
Into Each Life
Sinsatiable
What's Blood Got To Do With It?
Only In My Dreams
The House Husband
Cross Road
Forever Ain't Enough

<u>*Series Books*</u>

Beautiful Ugly
True Beauty (*sequel to Beautiful Ugly*)

<u>*My Son's Wife Series*</u>
My Son's Wife: The Beginning (Book 1)
My Son's Ex-Wife: Aftershock (Book 2)
My Son's Next Wife (Book 3)
My Sister My Momma My Wife (Book 4)
My Wife My Baby…And Him (Book 5)
The McCoy's of Holy Rock (Book 6)
Dem McCoy Boys (Book 7)
My Brother, Father…And Me (Book 8)
My Truth, My Time, My Turn (Book 9)

<u>*Adverse City Series*</u>
The Real Housewives of Adverse City
The Real Housewives of Adverse City 2

The Real Housewives of Adverse City 3
The Real Housewives of Adverse City 4

Anthologies
Bended Knees
Weary to Will
Learning to Love Me

Nonfiction
A Christian's Perspective: Journey Through Grief

ISBN:-13: 978-1-944643-20-1
ISBN: 10: 1-944643-20-6

Library of Congress Control Number: 2019901820

His Pen Publishing, LLC
www.hispenpublishing.com

My Truth
My Time
My Turn

My Son's Wife Series

Shelia E. Bell

*"The only way to win with a toxic person
is not to play."* Law of Attraction

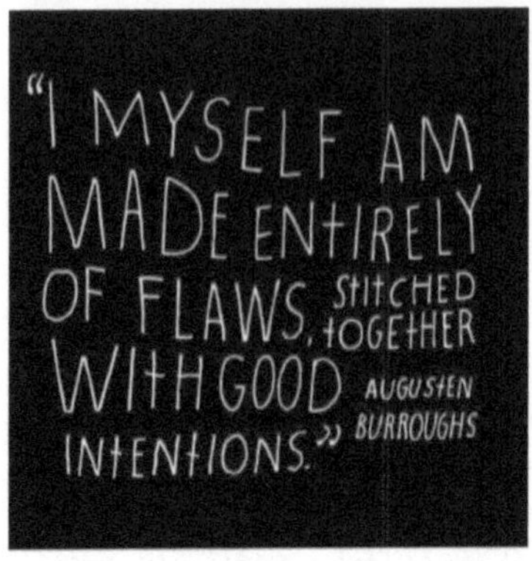

To all who follow my literary journey—I appreciate each and every one of you. I've said it before, but I must say it again: *there is no me without you!*

I thank God for blessing me, showing favor in my life, for never forsaking me and for giving me this gift to write and share these incredible stories.

To my mother, thank you for supporting me without fail. To my sons, grandsons, and great grands, I love you and hope my literary works will be part of my legacy that I leave to you. To my beautiful niece, Shante', thank you for believing I am perfect in spite of my many flaws. I love you so much.

Always keep your heads up, even when you feel like you aren't living the life you desire or achieving the dreams you had planned. Remember, sometimes what we think has escaped us in this life really has not. Oftentimes we fail to see how blessed and beneficial our lives are to those we encounter on this daily walk, run, and trot through life.

Oh, and to my ride or die, Rogue—the best cat and companion in the universe. We've been on some amazing journeys together. Thank you, Rogue for joining me on the ride.

I love you all!

Shelia E. Bell
—God's Amazing Girl

1

*"Sometimes you just want to slap people. Then
you remember Karma hits twice as hard."*
Unknown

*F*ancy scrolled through her phone and
stopped when she saw the BREAKING NEWS
headlines.

**FORMER SENIOR PASTOR OF HOLY ROCK MINISTRIES
ARRESTED ON FELONY EMBEZZLEMENT....**

She read the article over and over, not
believing Hezekiah had been carted off to jail.
Yes, she and her sons had discussed this. Part
of her knew this day was forthcoming, but to
actually read it, see it in black and white, made
her feel some type of way. She got ready to call
Khalil but stopped abruptly when she heard
Winston coming out of the bathroom.

Walking over to her with a white towel
covering his intimate parts, his body glistened
from having been underneath the streaming jets
of water.

Dang, this man is sexy. Full lips, strong chin,
cheek muscles that stood out when he clenched
his jaw. Fancy eyed him with desire in her eyes
as he approached her and stood in front of her.

He came close, looking down at her intensely,
before leaning down, and kissing her as she sat
on the edge of the firm bed. "I wish I could have

persuaded you to join me. I would have made it worth your while," he teased as he planted delicate kisses along her face, neck, and earlobes.

For a minute, Fancy forgot all about Hezekiah and his woes and allowed her mind and body to react to Winston's touch.

Your son is calling. The special ringtone pulled her back to reality before she could respond to Winston. Gently, she eased Winston back and answered it.

"Ma, did you hear? They got the dirty dog," Khalil said without saying hello. She could hear the satisfaction filtering through his voice.

"I know; I just saw it on my phone. I...I don't know what to say."

Winston looked down at her and listened, trying to decipher as much as he could about what Khalil could be saying. George had already contacted him and told him what had happened so he wasn't surprised if that was what Khalil was calling his mother about.

"What do you mean you don't know what to say? The man has gone down and it's not over. It's just beginning. Payback is a mutha, Ma. It's time he pays the piper. Know what I mean?"

"Yes, I hear you but it's still your father and my husband."

"Hold up, he is *not* your husband. You are divorced, Ma. And last I heard and saw for myself, you already got somebody to take his place. As for him being my father, yeah, he's my father by blood, but what's blood got to do with it? Apparently nothing, 'cause look at the way he's dissed me and Xavier. The man is ruthless, so don't go soft on me now, Ma."

"Yes, I hear ya, son. Anyway, I just need a minute. I'll call you back later. Okay?"

"Uh, okay, but you gonna be all right? I wasn't expecting you to sound like you just buried the guy or something. Everything'll be a'ite. You hear me?"

"Yes, sweetheart, I hear you. I'll talk to you later."

"Okay, bye, Ma." The call ended and with tears in her eyes, Fancy looked up at Winston.

"What is it, if you don't mind me asking?"

"It's Hezekiah."

"Is he all right? Did something happen? Another stroke?"

Fancy shook her head. "No, he's been arrested. It's been in the making for some time, but now that it's actually happened I...I don't know how I'm feeling," she admitted, wringing her hands and bowing her head.

Winston reached down, gathered her by her forearms, pulled her up against his taut body, and held her tightly as she rested her head against his chest. "The man was your husband until a few weeks ago. You have history together, children together. It's normal to have mixed emotions about his arrest."

Fancy looked up at Winston. "Thank you, Winston."

"I'm here for you. In any way I can. I hope you know that."

Fancy nodded her approval and laid her head back against his chest as he tightened his arms around her. She needed to feel safe, protected, and secure. Winston made her feel all of the above.

Winston's mind was a whirlwind of conflicting thoughts. He had not admitted to himself until now his growing feelings for Fancy McCoy. She reminded him of his ex, Josselyn. He and Josselyn had been engaged for less than six months when she, out of the blue, called off the engagement, saying she wasn't ready to get married after all. Winston was heartbroken. When she accepted his proposal of marriage it was like a dream had become a reality. It was heartbreaking for him to see her weeks later with another man when they were supposed to spend their lives together, but life had offered a cruel blow.

The caveat in the whole break up was when Winston received a promotion on his job that would require him to relocate to Memphis. After ending things the way she did, Winston couldn't wait to leave town and start anew.

His mind was not on meeting anyone else. Instead, his intentions were to make a mark in his new position in Memphis and continue to move up the corporate ladder. But his chance encounter with Fancy revealed just how small of a world it is.

Not exactly a guy with a stellar reputation behind closed doors, it didn't take much prodding from his longtime friend, George Reeves, when Winston told him about the hot woman he'd met at Brother Juniper's restaurant. George asked Winston to tell him more about the woman who seemed to have temporarily gotten his mind off Josselyn. George broke out into raucous laughter when Winston told him the woman's name was Fancy McCoy. How much better could things get?

George gave Winston some background on Fancy McCoy and her husband, Hezekiah. He didn't want his friend getting sucked in by the likes of any one with the last name 'McCoy', but it could possibly work for George the more he thought about it.

Listening to George run down a quick history about the McCoy's and Holy Rock made Winston that more enthralled and eager to get to know more about this striking mystery woman he'd met.

As for George, the more he gave thought to Winston's encounter with Fancy, the more he convinced himself this was divine intervention. Why else, of all the women he could have met, Winston met Fancy McCoy? From there, a plan began to circulate in his mind. If he could convince Winston to woo Fancy McCoy, and if she liked Winston, then Winston could keep his eyes and ears open for any shenanigans she and her crooked sons might have up their sleeves toward Hezekiah, and possibly toward George too. In return for his spying, George would only need to convince Winston he could enjoy the pleasure of having a knock off like Fancy to mess with since he'd made the move to Memphis and didn't know a lot of people.

If George was able to get the inside scoop on Fancy's plans, the less he would have to worry about his money train being cut off by Hezekiah. George figured it would be a win-win for both him and Winston. Of course, he'd break off a little money to Winston from time to time, not that Winston needed it. The man enjoyed a lucrative career and money was the least of his worries.

After some prodding, with a bit of reluctance mixed with curiosity, Winston agreed to get to know Fancy better. Anything Winston heard or saw that he believed might be helpful in their pursuit of the money George told Winston Hezekiah's son had stolen from his dad, Winston was supposed to let George know.

What took Winston by surprise was his feelings. He didn't expect to develop the strong attraction he had toward Fancy, but he did. She was easy to like, made him laugh, and definitely made him forget about Josselyn breaking his heart. But was it enough to make him back off doing what he had agreed? He tried not to think about that but every time he thought about telling George he wasn't on board with the plan anymore he remembered how he had been walked over by Josselyn, and he knew he could not fully trust Fancy. Thus, his loyalty remained with George.

"Look, everything will be fine. You're going to be fine," Winston assured Fancy. To see how much she was affected by Hezekiah's arrest told Winston a lot. Fancy still loved her husband. *What a fool this Hezekiah guy is.* It also told him something else—to keep his heart in check because her feelings certainly didn't lie with him.

2

"When I look at you I lose my sense of being. Is this love?" Tapan Ghosh

*E*liana stretched, slowly opened her eyes, and turned in the bed. She smiled in contentment when she saw Khalil lying next to her, sleeping soundly, with an ever so slight snoring coming from his throat. She took it to mean he was resting well. This made her happier than ever. As she eased up in the bed, being extra careful not to wake him, memories of the night before played on repeat in her mind and a warm glow flowed through her.

She and Khalil had been involved in an intimate relationship for months now. Her spirit convicted her, telling her it was wrong for her to be sleeping with her boss who was also her pastor. Yet, her heart overruled every time Khalil pulled her into his arms.

Eliana had been involved in one serious relationship prior to Khalil but that was when she was in high school. It lasted through her freshman year in college, but in the end the distance proved to be too great to sustain the relationship. He found someone else and she went on to concentrate on her college curriculum where she dated on and off. After graduating, she went straight into work mode while continuing to pursue a master's in Biblical studies. Having graduated a few months ago, she could now focus on her career at Holy Rock—and Khalil McCoy.

With her educational goals realized, her next major goal was to become First Lady Eliana McCoy. If she could get Fancy back in her corner and on her side it would give her more leverage.

"Hey," Khalil said, waking up and kissing Eliana on the side of her face as he opened his eyes and gathered her underneath his right arm. "What time is it?"

"Almost eight."

Hearing that, Khalil sat up in the bed, swiveled his long, muscular legs around until they connected with the cold hardwood floor.

"I've got to get up. I have to pick up Stiles at ten."

"No, actually you don't. Your mother is going to pick him up."

Looking back and over his shoulder he eyed Eliana curiously. "What are you talking about? And how do you know that? She didn't' mention it and I talked to her early this morning."

"She told me last night before I left midweek service. She said she was going to call and let you know."

"Well, she didn't." Khalil became immediately irritated. Why hadn't she told him? Probably because she knew he wouldn't be on board with that little move of hers. He still didn't feel comfortable with his mother having a relationship with his uncle. Something between those two just didn't sit right. "Where's my phone?"

"It's—"

"Never mind. I know where I put it." He opened the drawer to the bedside table and retrieved it. Without saying anything else, he called his mother.

"Good morning, sweetheart."

"Ma. What's this I hear about you picking up Stiles?"

"Oh, I forgot to tell you when we talked last night. I was so wrapped up in what's going on with Hezekiah. Anyway, I talked to Stiles earlier yesterday and I told him I would pick him up. I live closer to the airport than you so it's no big deal. We're going to have a late breakfast and then head to the church afterward. You can meet him there and go over everything you need to with him. I know you two have a lot of ground to cover. I told Eliana. Didn't she tell you? I mean, she *is* your personal assistant. Seems like she would have removed that from your calendar." Fancy was fishing. She was nobody's fool. She purposely told Eliana she would tell her son about her plans but she really had no intention of doing so until the last minute. She wanted to see if Eliana would tell him herself. Though she had no concrete proof, she felt in her spirit that Khalil and Eliana were sleeping together. It wasn't that she minded, not at all, especially now that Pepper had managed to get Xavier's mind off that twit brother of Eliana's. Plus, as long as Eliana could keep Khalil interested, the less he would have time to mess around with the other nitwitted females running around Holy Rock trying to snag her son. Not to mention Detria Graham. She was a whole other story. But she hadn't heard Khalil mention

Detria's name in a while, so maybe she was already out of the picture. God knows, she hoped so. That woman was nothing but trouble. She'd caused enough upset in her family by messing around with both Hezekiah and Khalil. How nasty was that?

"Look, Ma. I've told you before, chill. I got this. I don't need you trying to take up my slack like I'm a li'l boy or like I'm my brother. Things are good and I've learned a lot as senior pastor. I can handle my business, personal and church business. You feel me?"

"That's not what I was doing, Khalil. Stiles is my friend and he's my brother-in-law. He's family so what's wrong with that?"

"I'm telling you, I don't like this cozy little friendship you two got going on."

Fancy shifted from one leg to the other as she stood in the kitchen of her home. "Khalil, please. What are you talking about? Stiles has become a good friend and I know you can't think he has something more than friendship on his mind, or me either for that matter, cause if you do then you're sadly mistaken." She threw one hand off in the air, shook her head as if he could see her and then rested her elbow on the kitchen island.

"Where's that guy, uh, Winston anyway? He still coming around? I haven't seen him since you threw that party and that was months ago. He out or what?"

"No, I'm still seeing him. He's been coming to church. Not every Sunday, but he's been there."

"I haven't seen 'em."

"That's because he sits in the back. He doesn't want to sit up front where I sit and that's fine with me. You have too much on your mind on Sundays so it's not like you would notice him out of the thousands of people pouring into Holy Rock."

Khalil smiled when his mother made mention of the number of people attending Holy Rock. She was right. Every Sunday, at every service, the church was filled to capacity. The TV ministry was booming and the livestreaming had thousands of viewers. He had little, if anything, to complain about.

"Anyway, I've got to finish getting ready. I'll see you at church later. And don't worry; I won't keep Stiles out all afternoon. Just gonna feed him and bring straight to you. Are you okay with that, son?" Fancy waited for his reply.

"Yeah, whatever, Ma. I'll see you later."

"Okay, baby. Love ya."

"Love you too."

"You feel better now?" Eliana crawled across the bed, planted her body behind his, and encircled her arms around his neck. Kissing him lightly on his shoulders and ears, she tenderly turned his head so they were face to face.

Khalil quickly forgot about the conversation with his mother and instead placed his focus on the beautiful being next to him. "Might as well make good use of this extra time since I don't have to pick up Stiles, huh?"

"Sounds good to me."

"What do you have in mind?" Khalil asked.

"I can show you better than I can tell you."

"Umm, is that so?" Khalil pushed her back on the bed. Parting her lips, she let him possess her mouth as they picked up where they'd left off the night before.

A half hour later, his phone rang while Eliana was in the bathroom. He answered it when he saw it was Detria, though his first mind was to ignore the call. But he knew Detria. If he ignored it, it would only make her call him again, and again, and again.

"Yo."

"Hey, what's up?"

"I don't know. You tell me."

"I miss you. I haven't seen you in weeks. You're always telling me you're busy."

"That's because I am, Dee. What you been up to?"

"Thinking about you. I want to see you. Will you come by later?"

He looked toward the master bathroom to see if Eliana was coming out. She wasn't. Faucet water was still running. He could hear it clearly. "Nah, don't think so. Your ex will be here in a coupla hours so I'll be spending all day, and probably most of the evening, getting him settled."

"Say what? So he accepted your offer? That fool is moving back to Memphis?" She laughed into the phone. "Get outta here."

"He's not moving back, like in moving back full time. He's still going to pastor his church in Houston, but yeah he accepted the position. He'll be going back and forth. Either way, that ought to make you happy." Khalil teased, knowing that would set her off.

"You got me messed up. He can stay right where he is...in Houston. Ain't nothing he can do for me and it sure ain't nothing I can do for him. If I saw him on the street today, I'd walk right by his weak behind like he wasn't there."

This time Khalil laughed into the phone. "You're crazy. You know that?"

"Yeah, and you like it, don't you."

Khalil started to respond but stopped when he heard the water stop running. "Look, I gotta get outta here. Let me hit you up on my way to Holy Rock. Okay?"

"Yeah, but I want to see you. Don't let me down, Khalil."

"Yeah, sure, Dee. Later," and he ended the call.

He smiled as he thought about Detria. She could be sweet at times, but she was not for him. True, she'd helped him out a lot, a whole lot, but she wasn't the woman for him. Not only had she had an affair with his father, she was too much into drugs. She didn't think he was aware of her heavy drug usage, but he was. He just didn't say anything. There was evidence in her room almost every time he went to see her. He had lived the street life as a youth and dealt in drugs most of that time, so he was familiar with the various types of drug paraphernalia. He'd seen remnants of white powder on Dee's nightstand, saw paraphernalia inside the drawer but he said nothing. It really didn't matter much to him because Dee would never be a permanent fixture in his life. The fact she had a little boy she never seemed interested in seeing was another factor that made him know she would never be more than a means to get money and an easy lay. Any woman who could easily forsake her kid was not a woman he wanted to call his lady.

Now that things were going uphill with his ministry, and his pockets were being padded with money from that ministry, he was ready to put things to an end with Dee. Plus, though he had no proof, he felt like she was still in communication with his dad and he could never fully trust her.

The time had come for him to tell her to move on with her life. He had bigger dreams to chase and she wasn't part of them. It was time for him to make another move. Get a wife. And if he decided to keep a woman or two on the side, it still wouldn't be Dee.

Listening to Eliana singing in the bathroom, he thought, *She might be wifey material.* In some ways she reminded him of his mother. Eliana was beautiful, smart, loyal, and she knew church business inside and out. She could help him in a number of ways, plus she was good in bed. A little conservative, but he was slowly bringing her out of her coyness. Yeah, maybe she *was* the one to wear the title of First Lady.

3

"You can only be jealous of someone who has something you think you ought to have yourself."
Unknown

"I'm almost ready." Pepper strolled into the kitchen where Xavier was making himself a green smoothie. "I just have to finish doing my hair and we can get outta here."

"Cool. You sure you don't want me to blend you one? It won't take but a minute."

"I'm sure. I'll get something to snack on when I get to work. You know I'm not much of a breakfast person anyway."

Xavier finished blending the smoothie, poured it into a twenty ounce Yeti tumbler and placed the lid on it. He sat it to the side and then began dismantling the blender so he could wash it out when his text chimed.

"You at work yet?"

It was Ian. Xavier hadn't seen him in a couple of weeks, but Ian was persistent. At first, when he realized Xavier and Pepper were spending more time together and acting like a couple, Ian was beside himself. But as time passed, he had started calling and texting Xavier more, hoping to win him back.

Xavier washed the blender and put it away in the cabinet before replying to Ian's text.

"No, about to leave now. What's up?"

"How bout lunch?"

"Don't know about that. Got a busy day."

"Dinner?"

"Ian, like I said. IDK."

His phone rang. "I thought we agreed that we were friends. You don't have to brush me off every time I ask if we can hang."

"I'm not brushing you off, Ian. It's going to be wild at work today and the rest of the week. Stiles Graham is supposed to be in town in a couple hours so that means we're going to be in back-to-back meetings. I don't know what time I'll be free."

"I hear ya." Ian sighed into the phone. "He accepted the position?"

"Yea, I thought I told you."

"No, you didn't, and Eliana doesn't talk much about what goes on at Holy Rock unless I ask, and frankly I'm not that concerned about the happenings around that church. I'm only concerned about one person. You."

Pepper stood within earshot, but out of sight, listening to Xavier. She didn't have to listen but a second to know it was Ian on the other end. Why couldn't he just back off? She and Xavier were together now and there was no way she was going to let him ease back into Xavier's life.

"I'm ready, baby," she said extra loud, knowing darn well she rarely called him baby. That was just not her.

Ian instantly became angry but sucked in his breath and refused to say anything that would make Xavier know it. Instead he continued to talk. "I was thinking we could check out that concert downtown this weekend. Your favorite band is supposed to be on Mud Island for the Summer Jam Fest. You down?”

“This weekend?”

“Yeah. And my job gave me tickets so we wouldn’t have to pay to get in.”

“Uh, well, look. Yeah, okay, but we’ll talk about it later. I’ve gotta get to church.”

“Sure, talk to you later. Have a good one.”

“Thanks, backatcha,” and Xavier ended the call.

“So was that your little boyfriend, huh?” Pepper teased, walking up on Xavier and biting him lightly on his earlobe.

“Stop it already,” Xavier said, becoming a little uneasy with her teasing. “Ian and I are friends. I told you that I don’t know how many times. And, it’s not like you’re my girl.”

“Oh, is that right? Well what exactly am I? I mean we’re practically together every day. You’re sleeping with me. You seem to enjoy that part of this, whatever it is you don’t want to call it.” Pepper was offended and growing angry. She wanted Xavier all to herself, but Ian wouldn’t get out of the way.

“All I’m saying is you’re not the serious type, Pepper, and you know it. *And* you seem to forget one major factor.”

“And what is this so called major factor?” she said, folding her arms together and tapping her foot.

“I’m gay.”

She let out an explosive laughter and quickly stifled it by placing her hand over her mouth. “I’m sorry, did you just say you’re gay? Boy, please. You are not gay, Xavier. Not the way you've been smashing me these last few months."

"Well, maybe I'm bi. I don't know. All I do know is that until I can sort out my own life, I don't have time to add someone else into the equation. I...I'm still thinking about leaving Memphis anyway. I told you it was never my intention to stay here. Taking online courses is not satisfying to me. I always wanted to experience being away from home, living on a college campus. I had plans to do just that until all the stuff came up with my family."

Pepper shook her head. "You know what, Xavier, I guess you do need to sort out your life. You're one messed up guy. And if you ask me, I don't think you're bi. I think you're confused and you're scared. That person who molested you when you were a little boy really messed your mind up. Anyway, just take me to work. I'm done talking about this."

Pepper turned away from Xavier and walked toward the front door.

Xavier didn't say a word. He grabbed his keys off the kitchen counter and followed behind Pepper. Locking the door, still without saying a word, the two of them walked to his car.

Once inside the car, Xavier spoke. "I need my space."

"You got it." The remainder of the drive was in silence.

At Pepper's job, she got out of the car, turned around and said. "You got problems. Real problems. I thought we had something but you've made it clear that you are not feeling me. You want dude, so you can have him. I'm done,

Xavier." With that, she slammed the door with all of her force and stormed off.

Xavier sat in his car watching as Pepper walked away. Rubbing his hand across his bald head, he hit his hand against the steering wheel. Tears flooded from his eyes. He was full, full of anger, full of fear, full of uncertainty. He needed direction and guidance. He needed someone to talk to. "God, help me," he cried out. "Help me, please."

He reached for his phone and made a call. "I need to see you."

"Where are you?"

"I'm headed back home."

"Be there in fifteen." Ian ended the call with a smile of satisfaction appearing on his face.

"Listen, man, how many times have I told you to be who you are. Accept the truth, Xavier. You're gay. That's that on that. You're trying to act another way by messing off with Pepper, but you and I both know that you ain't feeling her."

Xavier didn't know what to think. All he felt was a flurry of indecisive thoughts playing over and over in his head. He liked Pepper. Liked her a lot. He'd never been with a woman before Pepper and the sex with a woman was out of this world. But the truth remained, something was missing. Was it Pepper and his relationship? Maybe it had nothing to do with the sex aspect of it. Pepper could be pushy, controlling, while at the same time she made him laugh. Then again, maybe Ian was right;

maybe he should accept that he was gay and leave Pepper alone. He felt more comfortable and at ease when he was around Ian. It was the same way he felt when he and Raymone were together. Raymone, he missed that guy still. He wondered how he was doing. He could barely stand to think about him for any length of time because the memories of that fateful day when he wrecked his car, leaving Raymone a quad, forever replayed in his mind. No matter how much he prayed and asked God to forgive him, Xavier had a hard time forgiving himself.

"I don't know, Ian. Right now I've got a lot to deal with. I like her. I know you don't want to hear that, but it's the truth."

Ian had to play his hand carefully if he planned to have Xavier to himself. Things between them were going good until Pepper showed up in Xavier's life. Now that she'd done whatever to upset Xavier, this was his opportunity to shine. To be the listening ear for the man he had fallen in love with.

Ian wrapped his arm around Xavier as the two of them sat on the sofa. "I'm not saying there's anything wrong with liking Pepper. She's probably a cool girl. The two of you can be friends. I mean, I have female friends, but I'm not confused about who I am and they aren't wasting their energy trying to change me. I've had females come on to me before, Xavier, but again, I am who I am."

Xavier turned to face Ian. "That's the problem, Ian. I don't know who I am. I'm so busy trying to live up to my family's expectations of me. I have a father who turned out to be a snake and a cheater. Not to mention he despises the fact that I'm gay. I have a brother who everybody loves and whose the ultimate ladies' man. He's charming, debonair, cogent, handsome, with plenty of swag. Everything I'm not. My mother wants me to be like him. Everybody wants something from me."

Xavier jumped up off the couch, put both hands on the side of his head and began to shake his head from side to side. "Ughhhh. How much more of this crap can I deal with?"

Ian stood up. "Look, take it easy. Let's leave this alone for now. Why don't we take a ride. It's beautiful outside and I don't have to be back at work for another hour. I told my manager I had an emergency to come up. A ride will relax your mind."

"I wish I could but I need to get to Holy Rock. I told you my uncle is coming in today. I have a lot to do. But thanks, Ian. I don't know what I would have done if you hadn't been able to come."

"I'm here for you, Xavier. Whenever you need me. That's what I want you to see. Who did you feel most comfortable talking to?"

Xavier looked at Ian. "Uh, you."

"That's right. It was me you called. Not your big brother, not your mama. It was me. And you know why? It's because you know I get you, Xavier. I know what you're feeling. I understand all those conflicting thoughts rushing through your mind, and I don't judge you. I care too much about you. All I'm asking is for you to give us another chance. Let's see where things can go. Let Pepper know that it was good while it lasted but you need some space."

"Look, I gotta go." Xavier walked toward the front door slowly.

"Yeah, me too. Come on, let's get outta here," Ian said, stepping in front of Xavier and opening the door.

Xavier turned and locked the door behind him then proceeded to walk to his car.

"I'm behind you, Xavier."

"I know and thanks for everything. I'll call you later after I leave Holy Rock."

"Sure."

They got inside their cars. Ian lingered, watching as Xavier drove off. He was pleased with the fact Xavier had turned to him. It was a good sign. He turned the ignition, put the car in drive, and sped off. Turning on the radio, he smiled as his favorite artist, Chris Brown, started singing his new song. It fit perfectly.

Xavier sat at the red light. The things Ian said made sense, but then again, why did he have such a hard time being who he was? Was this God trying to tell him that his desires for men were wrong? If so, then why did God make him this way?" He was unaware the light had changed to green until the car behind him honked its horn.

The phone rang. It was Pepper. He pushed the button on his steering wheel and answered. "What's up?"

"We need to talk. Can you stop by my place when you leave work?"

"I don't know, Pepper. I'm willing to bet it's going to be a long day. With Stiles coming in and all, we have a lot to get done."

"Just call me when you get home. I don't care how late it is. Okay?"

"Yeah, sure."

"You promise?"

"I said I would."

"Okay, talk to you later." Pepper ended the call.

She wasn't about to let things end the way they did this morning. She wanted Xavier for herself. At first when they met and she was told he was gay, she looked at him as one of her projects. Her mission was to get him into her bed and she had accomplished that. It had been easier than she thought it would be. But the more she hung out with Xavier, the more she fell for him. Now she believed she was in love with him. She had never told him and had only recently admitted it to herself. The way he made love to her was an indication to her that he was nowhere near being gay. She had to make him understand that. The only way she could bring him all the way over to her side was to be patient, more understanding, and whip it on him every chance she got. She laughed to herself as she sat in her small office cubicle in front of her computer, and muttered, "Game on, Ian."

Xavier hit the steering wheel with brute force when he took a quick glance on the front and back passenger floor and seats for his laptop case. "Dang! Now I have to go all the way back home." He drove a half block looking for a good place to turn around. He turned into the Target parking lot and drove until he could find space to make his turn to go back into the street in the direction of his apartment. He came to a crawl when he caught the side profile of a laughing couple as they casually sauntered in front of his vehicle. He thought about himself and wondered if he would ever experience a relationship filled with happiness and unconditional love. He looked closer as something about the couple looked familiar. He watched as they passed. He squinted his eyes, like he was unsure of what he saw. It was his mother's friend, Winston, engaged in deep conversation with none other than Detria Graham.

Xavier continued watching as Winston opened the passenger door for Detria and she climbed inside. A woman Xavier didn't recognize was sitting behind the steering wheel. Xavier picked up his phone and quickly took a couple of pictures.

Winston waved a goodbye as he closed Detria's door and began walking toward another car, which Xavier guessed must belong to him because he saw Winston open the door and get inside

Xavier drove forward. "Man, ain't that some...," he mouthed as he pulled out into the street and made the left turn. He quickly called his brother. "You'll never believe what I just saw."

"What's going on, bruh?"

"I'm sending you a picture now."

4

*"Holding on to anger is like grasping a hot coal
with the intent of throwing it at someone else; you
are the one who gets burned." Buddha*

*H*ezekiah, with the aid of a walker, stood on
his feet for several seconds. He inhaled then
exhaled, feeling quite pleased with his
accomplishment.

Both his physical and occupational therapists
had been working with him almost every day
since he'd been out on bond. His speech was
almost back to normal other than a few words
he had problems pronouncing. He was well on
his way to being the Hezekiah he was before his
stroke.

His prominent criminal defense attorney, one
of the best in the city, reassured him the federal
prosecutor would find it difficult, if not
altogether impossible, to prove to the jury that
he had embezzled money from Holy Rock. And if
they did, he told him he would argue to get him
probation at the most. Hezekiah would take
probation any day over sitting in a prison cell.
He had no desire to relive that kind of life. The
six years he and Fancy spent behind iron bars
had been enough to last a lifetime. Hezekiah had
made a promise to himself that he would never
return.

As he thought about the two days he spent in
jail until his arraignment and bond hearing, he

became angry. If it hadn't been for his family he wouldn't be dealing with a criminal case. He didn't need anyone to convince him otherwise. He would stake his life on it being Fancy and their sons.

Fancy knew the church books like the back of her hand and though she wasn't aware he had been embezzling funds from Holy Rock, no one was going to tell him that she didn't have some idea. Their lavish lifestyle certainly wasn't all the way due to what he was being paid by Holy Rock.

His limp wristed baby boy had smarts like his mother and he was a whiz in math and finances along with being computer savvy. He had probably been the brains behind doctoring the financial records at the direction of his scheming oldest son, Khalil, and slick-tailed, Fancy. Khalil was always a street smarts kinda kid and he used those same street smarts and know-how to turn his back on his own father.

Hezekiah stumbled and fell back in the chair planted behind him as he thought about his family's betrayal. What happened to blood being thicker than water?

"Be careful. Take your time," the physical therapist told him. "You've been doing remarkably well. If you keep this up, you'll be taking steps before you know it," the male PT added, "and then walking on your own."

"Now do you see why we keep that chair behind you? You have to build up the strength in your legs. You're blessed though because you've come a long way. There are many stroke victims who never regain their mobility," the second therapist said.

"Yeah, God knows I can't be bound to a wheelchair the rest of my life. I have too much to do. Too many scores too settle. Too many fires to put out. Know what I mean?" Hezekiah huffed.

Both therapists nodded.

Isabella walked into the room, halting the conversation. "Excuse me, I made spaghetti and meatballs for lunch. Do you want anything else to go with it?"

"Did you make garlic toast?"

"Yes."

"Anything green?"

"Yes, green beans."

"Okay, that's good."

"So, if you're done with your therapy I'll make you a plate now. That is if you're hungry."

"I'm sure he's worked up an appetite," the female therapist joked.

"Yep, I have."

"Well, don't let us stop you from lunch. We're done for the day," the male therapist stated. "We'll see you at ten o'clock Wednesday."

"Thanks."

"Keep doing the exercises we showed you."

"I will." Hezekiah escorted them to the door in his wheelchair. When he turned around, his eyes locked with Isabella's son. "He's growing fast isn't he?"

"Yep, he is."

"Isabella, we need to talk."

Isabella grew nervous. Was he going to stop taking care of her and her son? Would she have to go back out on the streets? It was hard to predict what Hezekiah had on his mind.

"What did I do?"

"You haven't done anything. Sit down for a minute."

Isabella, trembling, slowly sat in the living room chair.

"I think it's time you go into rehab. You know, get your life together. If you plan on being a good mother to him, you need to be sober. I'll pay for someone to take good care of him while you're there."

"I...I don't know. I don't want to leave my son with strangers to take care of him. Plus, I don't do as much drugs as I used to."

Hezekiah didn't know why he was having a tender moment for Isabella. Maybe it was his religious background. God had performed some miraculous things in his life in spite of his bad behavior. He felt convicted for treating Isabella the way he had. He'd rescued her from the prison of the streets only to make her his prisoner. The girl had a serious drug addiction. He could no longer avoid the fact that she needed help.

Isabella was a bright, loyal young lady. If given the right chance and the right opportunity, she could make something of her life. She was a great artist too. Hezekiah had discovered many of her drawings tucked away in a folder she left on the living room table one day.

"Think about it." He picked up the little boy and rode him into the kitchen.

Isabella fixed Hezekiah and her son a plate of spaghetti.

She removed the boy from Hezekiah's lap and placed him in his own chair.

It was rare that Hezekiah interacted with the kid, but the times he did, it made Isabella happy. All she wanted in life was to be loved and cared for. But for some reason love had always escaped her. Being at Hezekiah's beck and call was something she'd gotten used to but that wasn't to say she was happy with her living arrangements. Sure, he provided for her and her son, kept a roof over their heads, food in their bellies, and made sure she got the drugs her body craved. But she longed to live a normal life as a nineteen-year old. She wanted friends, not drug friends, but *real* friends. Girlfriends she could hang out with, go to the mall with, and do fun girl things. She wanted a real boyfriend, something she'd never had. She had been sexually molested when she was four years old. In the streets as a girl of twelve she'd been raped and assaulted and then turned to selling her body to survive. When Hezekiah took her off the streets she thought her life would be different, but he was really no better than the people who had used and abused her before he found her. He preached God but he lived the life of the devil. He could be sweet and kind but then mean and evil. He was like Dr. Jekyll and Mr. Hyde. He could change at the drop of a dime.

Today was a good day. Hezekiah was in a good, talkative mood.

"All I'm saying, Isabella, is it's your choice what you want to do with your life. If you want to make a change for the good, you need to get clean and sober. You can make a better life for you and your boy. I'm willing to help you, and God is a God of second chances, you know."

Isabella sat in the chair next to her son, watching him as he picked up the spaghetti noodles with his fingers and placed them inside his mouth.

"I'm not supplying you with drugs anymore, Isabella. That's what this amounts to. Now you can do this the easy way and go into rehab where they can help you with getting your system detoxed or you can do it the hard way and be sick, real sick while your body withdraws. But that will be tough on you and either way you won't be able to take care of your son."

"I don't want to use anymore. I've been doing drugs since I was twelve years old and on the streets. I do want to be here for my son." She began to cry softly. Looking at her, Hezekiah's heart softened. She looked like a little child. He'd made so many mistakes in his life, but this was one that he definitely regretted. How could he do the things he'd done to her and with her and then turn around and call himself a man of God? She wasn't the same as Detria. Detria was not someone he felt sorry for. Quite the opposite. Detria was a full grown woman who didn't give a rat's behind about her kid and who only cared about what she could get out of somebody. That's why he had no problem sleeping with her. He used her for what he needed. Maybe he was wrong about that, too, and if he was he would have to be a man, own up to it, and suffer the consequences of his actions. But that was another story. Right now he was fixated on doing what he could to help Isabella. It was time he set her free but he wouldn't be able to do that unless she was willing to get help.

"I'll go. Promise me though you'll get someone to take good care of my son."

"If it'll make you feel better, and help with your decision, I've been looking into a facility that provides single parents with children a place on the grounds for their kids to stay while the parent is going through rehab. Once you go through detox they allow you to spend time with your kid. But you'll have to be committed to this, Isabella. It's the one and only chance I'm offering."

"That would be good. Knowing my son is near me, I know I can do it. Thank you." She wiped her tears, jumped up from her chair and dashed over to Hezekiah. Wrapping her arms around his neck, she kissed him on the cheek. "Thank you, Hezekiah. Thank you so much."

"I'll make the necessary phone call and see when they can accept you. But you can't tell a soul that I'm behind this. Do you understand?"

"Yes, I promise. I won't say a word."

5

"They say, "Love doesn't cost a thing," but I disagree because falling in love with the wrong person could cost you everything." Amari Soul

"I met with Winston. He says everything is good between him and Fancy, but he wants you and George to know he's done."

"What do you mean he's done? He's not done until I say he's done."

"He's never met you and he says he doesn't want to meet you. He likes Fancy. That's the problem, Hezekiah. I think whatever you and George thought would happen has backfired in both of your faces. Fancy must have put some of that good-good on him." Detria laughed into the phone.

Hezekiah would never admit how much it bothered him at the thought of Fancy sleeping with another man. It had been George's idea, and Hezekiah admitted he never should have agreed to it. How could he blame Fancy for moving on with someone else when he'd mistreated her the way he had? But she didn't deserve brownie points either. Not after she and their sons accused him of embezzlement and now he was facing prison time. But to know that another man was falling for her and to know that man was an old friend of George's made him feel some type of way.

His life was spiraling out of control. He had to hurry up and get out of that wheelchair so he could get his life back, his church back, and pay back his ex and sons for all they'd done to destroy him. He had plans to come back stronger than ever.

As for Stiles returning to Holy Rock, that was another thing he had to contend with. He still couldn't accept the fact that Stiles was his brother and that the old man, Chauncey Graham, was his father. He would rather burn in hell than see Stiles win back Holy Rock. As for his father, he could rot in hell right beside him.

Pastor had reached out several times after it was revealed he was Hezekiah's father, but Hezekiah couldn't and wouldn't have anything to do with him. He hadn't been in his life all this time. No need to start now that Hezekiah was a grown man. That's one of the reasons he hoped Isabella would take advantage of his offer to send her to rehab. He didn't want her kid growing up without his mama or standing the chance of being taken away from her. The road Isabella was going down now would lead to destruction and he didn't want any parts of it.

"I need to meet him."

"I thought you said you didn't want to meet him. You said you were going to let George be the go to person."

"I don't need to be reminded of what I said, Detria. And how do you think George is going to see him? From behind bars?"

Detria shrugged. "I don't know. I'm just saying. Anyway, George will be released in a month or so."

"We're talking about now, not a month or so. Look, just set it up. I'll meet him at your crib. Tomorrow night. Seven thirty."

Detria huffed in the phone. "Whatever, Hezekiah. I'll call him and see what I can do, but I'm telling you now, I can't promise you anything."

"I don't care how you do it, just make it happen." He pushed the end button on his phone, followed by making another phone call.

"How's my kid?" he asked the woman who answered.

"What happened in jail that made you want to call me and ask about your child?" Bitterness rang throughout her voice, piercing his ear over the phone.

"I didn't call to argue. I asked you a simple question. How's my kid?"

Silence filtered through the phone.

"Hello?"

"He's good. Now, is that all? I have other things to do than to hold the phone with you, Hezekiah."

"I want to see him."

The woman laughed loudly. "Are you crazy? You haven't seen him since he was seven months old. He's three years old now and now you want to see him? I don't think so. All you need to do is keep that money coming in every month and we're straight. I don't bother you and you don't bother us."

"I want to see my son," Hezekiah repeated as if he didn't hear anything the woman said.

"And I said no." The phone went silent.

"Hello?" *Pause.* "Hello?" "Mariah?" He looked at his cell phone. The call had ended. He thought about calling her back but decided against it. He'd bide his time, perhaps wait until things were better for him physically. He was going to see his kid and he wasn't going to let Mariah stop him.

Mariah was another one of the women he'd messed off with during his tenure as senior pastor of Holy Rock. She used to belong to Holy Rock. That's where he met her. She was part of the Pastor's Aid Ministry. When they first started messing around, Mariah was married but her husband rarely, if ever came to church. She had two kids at the time. When she told him she was pregnant, Hezekiah didn't believe it was his kid, but she kept insisting it was his. She said she and her husband hadn't slept together for months. There must have been some truth to her story because soon after she got pregnant her husband left Mariah and took their two kids with him. Hearing that, Hezekiah insisted they take a DNA test. Bingo! Just like that, 99.9% chance the kid was his. Even Maury couldn't have beaten those odds.

Hezekiah saw his son twice. Once when he was three weeks old and again when he was seven months. His marriage to Fancy was still intact and he didn't want anything or anyone to come between it. He thought Mariah understood that so he didn't know why she would get herself knocked up. Sure, he was to blame too for sleeping with her without the added protection of a condom, but with her being married, he assumed she was still sleeping with her husband so he felt more relaxed doing it without a condom. If she got pregnant, or when she got pregnant, he automatically thought the husband would think it was his because it would be highly likely. But Mariah had left out the major detail that she and her husband weren't vibing like that and hadn't been since before she and Hezekiah started their affair.

The woman had become so possessive and stupid that she sent that fake Will to his house for Fancy to see and flip out. He had to be more careful in his selection of women.

Seeing Isabella's kid running around his house almost every day, gave him the desire to see his kid.

He dialed Mariah's number again.

"What do you want?"

"I want to see my son."

"Let me say this to you one more time. Leave us alone, Hezekiah. I don't need you messing up my life a second time. My husband and kids are back. I'm making a change in my life for the better. As far as the law goes, this is his kid, legally, anyway. He's forgiven me and he's accepted Jude as his own. So please, let it go Let *us* go. You can stop putting money in my account if that's what it'll take for you to leave us be. I don't care anymore. I just want to be left alone."

"You didn't want to be left alone when you sent that fake Will to my wife."

"That's because I was still stuck on stupid back then. But all that's in my past. I had an affair with you, got pregnant, lost my husband and my kids because of it. But God forgave me, my husband forgave me. I've been given a second chance and I've moved on."

"Seems like if you had moved on like you say you have, you would have stopped accepting my money. You would have told me this a long time ago."

"My husband and kids have been back less than a year. And no, I didn't go out of my way to tell you. Why should I? I figured the least you could do was pay me for tearing my life apart, and Jude is your son. Just because you haven't tried to be in his life doesn't mean you shouldn't provide for him. Anyway, you've been fighting your own demons, Hezekiah. And I came to the realization that my son didn't need to be part of your mess. I didn't like being the knock off then and I won't be a knock off now. Not to you. Not to any other man. So please, leave us alone. I've moved on with my life. If you insist on trying to see Jude, I promise I'll make your life a living hell. I know some of your dirty little secrets, Hezekiah. Remember that."

"Are you threatening me, Mariah?"

"No, I'm making a promise. Now, goodbye, and please don't ever call my number again." For a second time, she ended the call.

6

*"I'm ready to accept the challenge. I'm coming
home." LeBron James*

Fancy sat across from the table watching and listening to Stiles talk about his decision to return to Holy Rock as associate pastor.

"I prayed about it long and hard. Considering Pastor's health and aging, and my desire to stand behind the pulpit of Holy Rock again, I guess you can say the decision was made for me. I just hope I've listened and heard God correctly."

"I think you made the right decision." Fancy picked up her glass of diet soda and took a couple of swallows before sitting the glass back on the table. "I know it's going to be good for Holy Rock and for Pastor too. Many of our long time members who were there when you were pastor can't wait to see you grace the pulpit again." She gave him a reassuring smile.

"It's not like I'll be preaching every Sunday, but I must admit, it does feel good to be back. Just knowing that I have another opportunity to make Pastor smile again and of course continue to do God's will, makes me one grateful man."

Fancy nodded in agreement. "Well, looks like you're done eating, so what do you say we head on over to Holy Rock. That son of mine has been texting me like crazy asking where we are."

"Didn't you tell him we were going to stop to have some lunch?"

"Yes, I did, but he's anxious to get this ball officially off the ground, and I can't say I blame him."

Fancy insisted on covering the check. After paying, they left the restaurant and headed to Holy Rock.

"Welcome, Pastor Graham. Good afternoon, Sista Fancy," the front office receptionist greeted them as they entered Holy Rock.

Eliana saw them approaching and called Khalil in his office to let him know Stiles and Fancy had arrived. Once that was done, she got up and walked around from behind her desk. "Welcome back to Holy Rock, Pastor Graham. Pastor Khalil wants you to wait in the small conference room. He'll be with you shortly. I'll take you there."

Fancy threw up one hand. "No need, Eliana. I've got this."

"Oh, yes, ma'am, but Pastor Khalil asked for you to give him a few minutes. He's in a meeting." Eliana returned to her desk with an unpleasant look on her face while Sista Mavis strained to hear every word. Her desk and the other admins' desks were behind a glass petition. They could see anyone who came through the front doors and hear most of what conversations transpired.

"While we wait on him to get free let me show you to your office," Fancy said to Stiles. "Come this way." She turned, looked at him, and waved him toward her as she walked up the hall. "Oh, Eliana, when the pastor is done, will you tell him we'll be in Pastor Stiles' office."

"Yes, I sure will, Sista Fancy."

After Fancy and Stiles walked up the hallway and were out of sight, Sista Mavis approached Eliana's desk.

"He's good looking isn't it?"

"Excuse me?"

"Pastor Stiles is one good looking man, isn't he? And you know he's single. He needs a good woman. I know you're young but in this day and time, age ain't nothing but a number. I believe you would make him a good wife. God knows that poor man has had his share of bad luck."

"Yes, he's handsome, but I'm not interested in Stiles Graham." Eliana stood, picked up a stack of folders off her desk, walked six feet, and put them inside the file cabinet.

"Humph, I think you'll have a better chance at snagging him rather than Pastor K."

Eliana turned around, rolled her eyes at Sista Mavis, and then sat back at her desk. "I don't know what you're insinuating, but I have no interest in Pastor K, as you call him." Hearing what Sista Mavis said was rattling. Was it that obvious she had feelings for Khalil?

"Chile, please, I wasn't born yesterday. Even a blind woman could see you got a thang for that boy. And I can't say I blame you. He's just as good looking as his daddy and his uncle, but he's not ready to settle down. That boy may be the senior pastor of this church, but he's still got wild hairs all up...well you know what I'm saying. You seem like a decent girl. I wouldn't want to see you get hurt. Take my advice; set your sights on someone attainable. And it's sho not Pastor K. That's all I'm saying."

"Thanks but no thanks for that bit of advice. And I don't mean to sound disrespectful, Sista Mavis, but I don't discuss my personal business with my co-workers. Now, if you'll excuse me, I'm going to lunch. I'll forward the calls to you. Oh, and Pastor Khalil will be in and out the remainder of the day. He has quite a bit of ground to cover with Pastor Graham to get him settled."

Sista Mavis shook her head. "You young folks don't want to listen, but you do you, boo. Do you." With that being said, Sista Mavis waltzed back to her desk.

"I should have known it was something about dude," Khalil said as he looked at the image of Detria and Winston again. "And that wench, Detria, is nothing but a snake. Did you hear anything they said?"

"Nah, but they didn't act like they were strangers. I can tell you that. I don't know what's up but we need to find out," Xavier said. "I don't want Ma being messed over by this guy. It's bad enough she's forced to deal with Dad and all of his drama."

"Don't worry, I'm going to get to the bottom of this, but I can't right now. Eliana said Ma and Stiles are here. You have the paperwork he needs to read and sign?"

"Yeah."

"Keys to his spot?"

"Yea, I got you. Everything is straight. I'm just curious about this dude, Winston, and of all people for him to be with, Detria?"

"Like I said, let me handle it. And don't say a word to Ma about this."

"You know I won't."

The brothers walked out of Khalil's office and headed up the hallway.

After dismissing Sista Mavis' remarks, Eliana went outside and sat inside her car for a few minutes before driving to the nearby strip mall where there were several restaurants and a deli. She chose the deli. After placing her to-go order, she returned to her car with her food and sat inside of it eating and thinking about what Sista Mavis had said. No way was she interested or attracted to Stiles Graham. She'd seen the man a few times and he seemed to be a nice man, but he was about the same age as her parents. She wasn't into older men and especially men with as much baggage as she'd heard he had. No, she was not going to let anyone or anything keep her from building a strong relationship with Khalil.

Taking a bite of her veggie sandwich and then her fries, she thought about how Sista Fancy had all but brushed her aside like she was nobody—all because of her brother's relationship with Xavier. How could she control what two consenting adults did? Somehow, Fancy seemed to think she could. There was a time Fancy acted as if she liked Eliana but that wasn't the case now. What could she do to get Fancy back on her side? It wasn't rocket science, the fact was the closer she got to Fancy, the better the odds of getting Khalil to be all hers.

She finished eating her lunch and returned to Holy Rock. Driving up in the church parking lot, she spotted Khalil, Xavier, and Stiles getting into Xavier's car. Eliana already knew what the plans were for today. They were going to take Stiles to the house they'd leased for him. She was the one who had helped Khalil decide on it after he had been shown several houses. This one was located about seven miles from Holy Rock. It was a spacious four-bedroom brick bungalow in an upscale and quiet neighborhood. She believed he would like it. Holy Rock was also providing Stiles a 'company car' at his disposal for whenever he was in Memphis, plus many other perks.

After they drove off, Eliana remained in her car until it was time for her to go back inside. The day was still going to be a long one. There was an afternoon staff meeting where Stiles would be officially welcomed, and later the ministerial and office staff was supposed to join Pastor Khalil and Stiles for dinner. She couldn't wait until it all ended. Hopefully, afterwards, if it wasn't too late, Khalil would want to see her. Most of the time she came to his house because it was more private and out of the sight of his brother and her brother. Not that Khalil cared, or at least he said he didn't, but with a garage at his house, and it being inside a gated community, there was far less chance of nosy people seeing their comings and goings.

7

*"Whoever walks with the wise becomes wise, but
the companion of fools will suffer harm."*
Proverbs 13:20

*D*inner with Stiles and the staff was fun and informative. Stiles enjoyed all the special attention he received. He was made to feel truly welcome. He laughed, talked, got reacquainted with the staff and met the ministers and their wives or significant others.

His phone rang during dinner. He looked at the screen. It was Kareena. He ignored the call and instead shot her a quick text to let her know he was at dinner with the staff and would get back with her later.

"Stiles, tell the truth, do you like the spot we picked out for you?" Khalil asked.

"Yes, I love it. And it's not too far from Holy Rock, which makes it even better. It has more than enough space, the neighborhood is great. I have no complaints. None at all. God is good."

"Oh, yes he is," Fancy cosigned.

"Well, if you have any concerns or if we've missed anything, just let Eliana know. She'll be your administrative assistant as well. Sista Mavis will be her backup."

Stiles looked at the attractive young lady and showed his approval with a smile and a nod. "Yes, she told me. I promise not to be difficult, Sista Eliana."

"I'm not worried about that," Eliana said. "I'm sure I'll have no problem working with you."

Sista Mavis chuckled and then said, "You're going to love her. She's such a sweetheart. So smart and talented. I can't believe no one's snatched her up."

Eliana shot an eye at Sista Mavis and a fake smile. "In God's timing."

"That's right, baby," one of the ministers' wives said.

"I'm sure whoever God blesses to come into her life will be a lucky man," Fancy said, much to Eliana's pleasant surprise. Butterflies flurried in her belly as she quickly looked at Khalil.

"I agree," Khalil said.

At the end of dinner, Fancy told Stiles she would drive him home. They were going to pick up his leased vehicle the following day.

"Ma, Xavier is going to take him. It's getting late. You can just go on home."

Fancy gave Khalil a side eye. "Oh, okay. But I don't mind."

"I know, Ma, but I got it," Xavier said.

When Stiles arrived home and entered his new space, the first thing he did was take off his shoes. After that he stretched out his long arms and released a roaring yawn. It was almost nine thirty. It had been a long day and he was beat. He looked around the house and made himself familiar with it. The second bedroom was made into a home office. The third bedroom was a man cave, and the fourth was a guest room. His master bedroom was spacious and relaxing. All of the furniture was to his liking and everything was arranged perfectly. All he needed to do was unpack his luggage but he would do that later. First things first. He went into the living room, sat down in the high back chair and exhaled.

Removing his cell phone from its holder, he called Kareena.

"Hi, there? Were you sleep?"

"No, not quite. How did everything go?"

"Good. I was given the royal treatment. I felt welcomed and my spot is sweet."

"Sounds good. I'm glad it's working out for you."

"Any fires to put out at Full of Grace today?"

"No, everything was business as usual."

"I'll have Eliana to send you my schedule when I get to the office tomorrow."

"Eliana?"

"Yes, she's Khalil's administrative assistant, but she's going to report to me as well."

"Okay, that'll be fine."

An uncomfortable silence filtered through the phone.

"Ummm, well, I guess I'm going to call it a night. I'm exhausted and I have another long day tomorrow."

"Okay, no problem. I'm going to do the same. Call or text me if you need me, Stiles."

"Sure thing. Gnite." He ended the call. Thoughts of Kareena saturated his mind. Why did he let her walk out of his life? What was wrong with him? He practically pushed her into the arms of River. He didn't care how good of a man River was, Stiles wanted Kareena for himself.

His phone rang, yanking him from his thoughts.

"Are you settled in?" Fancy asked.

"Yes, but I had some phone calls to make first."

"Well, I just wanted to say it again. Welcome back."

"Thank you, Fancy."

"I want you to call me if you need anything. I don't come in the office everyday like I used to."

"Is that by choice?"

"Somewhat," she said. "We didn't talk about it at lunch but Khalil feels that it's time I do me. You know what I mean?"

"I think I do."

"He's doing well in the ministry. Things are moving in the right direction. And he and Xavier have things running pretty smoothly. Khalil doesn't want me involved as much because of the situation with Hezekiah."

"Speaking of my brother, any word from him lately?"

"No. All I know is he's out on bond. We did find out he lives somewhere in Arlington. At least, that's what we were told. I don't know how much truth there is to it."

"How do you feel about it?"

"About what? Him living in Arlington or his arrest?"

"His arrest?"

"I don't know, Stiles. I mean, I don't wish that for anybody. Me and Hezekiah know what it's like to spend time behind bars. We did six years.

Six years away from our kids, our family. Yes, I know it was because of our own making, but it's still something that I wouldn't wish on anyone. Maybe I shouldn't feel the way I do about it, but I do. I haven't said anything to the boys about my feelings. I mean, I was the one who was in their corners when they talked about reporting the embezzlement. I just don't know. Part of me feels guilty about it and the other part; well the other part of me doesn't know how to feel."

"That's understandable. I've told you before, love doesn't just disappear at the drop of a dime, especially when you have the history you and Hezekiah have. It just doesn't work like that. Believe me, I know from experience."

Fancy listened in silence. She could feel Stiles' sincerity over the phone. "Are you still in love with Detria?"

"What? Detria? Heck, no!" Stiles yelled before he knew it. "Sorry, but no way. I have regrets about the way things turned out for me and my first wife. You would've liked Rena."

"I remember seeing her. She was a beautiful woman. Have you ever thought about trying to get back with her?"

"Nah, she's moved on with her life. Has a husband and a bunch of kids. Plus, after the Jubilee Tragedy she made it clear my family was not welcome in her life. I can't say I blame her. Not only did I hurt her when we were married, but for her parents to be slaughtered by the woman who I learned was my mother? That's a whole other painful memory she has to deal with. Then my sister and her husband were killed too. I don't know how much more my heart can take. It literally aches with the weight of grief. Now my father may be in the first stages of dementia. My brother, your ex, doesn't want anything to do with me." Stiles paused. "Look, enough about me. That's not the road I was intending to go down. I just want you to know that I understand, Fancy. That's all I'm saying. Now that I'll be in Memphis more often, I hope we can spend more time together."

"Me too. I think we need each other to lean on."

"Yea, but you got dude in your life. What's his name?"

A bubble of laughter rose in her throat. "Winston."

"He's a lucky guy."

Fancy didn't know how to accept Stiles' remark. Was he flirting or just being friendly? She settled on the latter. Stiles had not shown any interest in her. Apart from the kiss, which she initiated that night long ago, he hadn't given her any indication that he wanted to be anything more than friends and in-laws. Anyway, she had Winston and she was happy in the relationship. He treated her with kindness and respect. He enjoyed wining and dining her and he was an excellent lover. Yet, her mind always fell back to Hezekiah. She had to keep reminding herself that everything she and Hezekiah shared was in the past.

"Thank you, Stiles. You know, it feels good to have someone to talk to. Someone who I don't have to put on airs with, who I can tell how I feel without being thought of as stupid or naïve. You get me, and I'm grateful for our friendship."

"Yea, the same here."

"What about the woman back in Houston. Karen? Is that her name?"

"It's Kareena. She's getting married."

"What? But I thought the two of you...well, I thought you two had something going on."

"I don't think I actually came out and said that, but either way I couldn't chance hurting her. I'm not ready to get into another relationship, you know. She's a good woman, a real good woman. I can't say I like the fact she's marrying someone else, but I couldn't expect her to sit around and wait on me. God knows I may never be ready to give my all to someone else again. I'm committed to my ministry. Full of Grace and Holy Rock. The man she's engaged to is a good man. A member of my church. And he's closer to her age."

"I see," Fancy said, hearing the hurt in Stiles' voice. "You need someone in your life, Stiles."

"I have God."

"You know what I mean."

"Yeah, I know. It's just like the young lady at dinner said when Sista Mavis talked about her not being married yet. She said in God's timing. That's how I feel. If it's meant for me to have another wife, it will be up to God. Everything happens according to his timetable. Not ours. Anyway, enough of us wallowing in our sorrows. I think I'm going to hit the shower and then see how that bed feels. It's calling my name."

Fancy laughed again. "I hear you. It was good talking to you, Stiles, and welcome back."

8

*"Never trust all of what you see, because
sometimes lies appear clearer than the reality."
Unknown*

"Hey, sweetheart. I didn't know you were coming over. You didn't call me. Wait, did I miss your call?" Detria turned around to retrieve her phone off the table in the family room.

Ignoring her, Khalil went straight to interrogating her. He wanted answers and he wanted them now. "How do you know Winston Washington and who is he to you?"

"Hold up, who and what are you talking about?" Detria asked, feigning surprise.

"Don't play me, Dee. You know darn well who I'm talking about, but since you wanna play dumb, this is who I'm talking about." He pushed his phone in front of Dee's face, revealing the picture of her and Winston. "Does this jog your memory? Now who is he to you?"

"He...he's a friend. Where did you get this picture?" A hollow feeling formed in the pit of her stomach.

"Don't worry about that. Now I'm going to ask you one more time, who is he?" Khalil grabbed hold of Detria's arm tightly.

"Khalil, stop it. You're hurting me."

He turned her loose, but she saw the anger in his eyes. It was like his face had darkened and his eyes had turned deep red. She rarely saw

51

him get this upset with her. "I told you, he's a friend. I was out shopping and I ran into him. We go way back."

"Why do I know you're lying?"

"I'm not. I'm telling you the truth."

"You're lying. But you know what, I'm not going to entertain your crap tonight, Dee, but I guarantee you this, I'm going to find out what connection he has to you." Khalil's steps reverberated with force across the hardwood floors as he made his way toward the front door.

"Khalil, wait. Don't leave. Please." She ran after him. "I miss you, baby."

Khalil didn't bother to stop until he got to Dee's front door.

"What if I told you Winston and Hezekiah are supposed to be meeting here at seven thirty tomorrow night? You can come over. Pretend you popped up. Then you can find out for yourself what's going on. I promise, I don't know anything they're doing. All your father told me to do was arrange the meet up. I promise, Khalil. Please, come back inside. I miss you, baby." A faint flush tinged her cheeks.

Khalil turned, looked at her. His eyes were hard and scornful. Deep creases formed on his face. "Remember this one thing, Dee. I'm my father's son. Don't play with me." With that being said, he stormed out of her door, not bothering to close it behind him.

Dee stood in the doorway, trembling. When she saw Khalil get in his car and drive off, she closed the door and ran back to the family room. Picking up her phone, she dialed the number. "Hezekiah, Khalil saw me talking to Winston."

"You're so stupid. How did that happen?"

"I...well, I had some shopping to do so I called him and told him to meet me so we could talk. I told him what you said about wanting to meet him." She pushed a hand through her hair. "He asked about George, and wanted to know the reason you wanted to see him. When I convinced him to come to my house tomorrow night, everything was cool. I don't know when Khalil saw us, but he did because he had a picture of me and Winston in his cell phone. I can't believe the first time I've laid eyes on that man and I end up getting caught up in more of your mess. I'm telling you this one last time, Hezekiah. After tomorrow night, I'm done. I'm not doing any more of your dirty work. I'll find me another supplier. I have money and I don't need you to do anything for me," she cried.

"You talk a good game now, Detria, but I know you. Frankly, I don't care if I never see your face again. And you finally make sense. I think it *is* time you and I part ways. You're more trouble to me than you're worth. After tomorrow night, I want you out of my life." Hezekiah ended the call.

He was furious. Sleeping with Detria had been a mistake from the start. All she caused was more problems for him and he was sick and tired of her. She was right, tomorrow night would be the end of it all. She could add nothing to his life.

After the day's events, and ending it with a deep conversation with Stiles, Fancy felt an overwhelming desire to pray. Most of the time she prayed out loud when she was home alone, rarely getting on her knees. But tonight was different. Stiles had made so much sense in the things he'd said.

Fancy knelt beside her bed. Clasping her hands together and looking upward, she began to pray. She asked God to first forgive her for all the wrong she'd done, for all the problems she'd caused in her own life and the lives of others. Hot tears welled into her eyes as she cried out to God. She didn't know how long she remained on her knees, but when she opened her eyes, a feeling of release and perfect peace washed over her as she got up and climbed into the bed. Pulling the soft white linen covers around her, within minutes she was asleep.

Before she knew it, morning had come. She opened her eyes, yawned and stretched then got out of bed. "Thank you, God." Wiping the sleep from her eyes, she stumbled to her bathroom and turned on the shower.

The streaming water added to the peace and calm in her spirit. She remained in the shower until the water began to turn cold. Stepping out, she quickly grabbed a towel off the towel rack to dry herself, when she heard her cell phone ringing. While continuing to dry off, she walked out of the bathroom and into her bedroom to retrieve the phone. The call ended before she made it to the phone. Picking up the phone, she looked at the missed call. It was Winston. This brought a smile to her face.

She finished drying off and then sat in the bed chair next to the night stand. "Good morning," she said while toweling her hair.

"Hey, sexy. I didn't mean to wake you from your beauty sleep."

"You didn't. I was actually in the shower when you called."

"Ummm, what I wouldn't give to be there with you."

Fancy blushed.

"So, Mr. Washington, how are you this morning?"

"I'm good. I'm at the office. I thought I'd call before I got too busy. I was thinking maybe you'd like to meet me for lunch."

"I'd love to. Where and what time?"

"I have two meetings this morning that I already know are going to be pretty lengthy so let's say one o'clock?"

"One is fine. Where do you want to meet?"

"I was thinking we could meet at Casablanca, the Poplar location."

"Oh, great. I love Casablanca. Their food is delicious. I'll be sure to save my appetite." She laughed into the phone.

"Good, then I'll see you at one. Have a good morning, sweetheart."

"Thanks, Winston. See you later."

She laughed, tossed the towel from her hair to the side, and twirled around. She liked Winston. Liked him a lot. She prayed out loud. "God, whatever you want this to be let it be. You know I like him, and I know I need to move on from any hopes of me and Hezekiah getting back together. So, God, if Winston is the man for me, then make it clear, but if he isn't, then remove him from my life."

Since she wasn't going into the office she called her girlfriend, Tara. Tara was a stay-at-home mom. Fancy knew Tara worked out almost every morning at the Y near where they lived.

"Hey, girl."

"Hi, Fancy."

"You working out today?"

"You know it. I'm getting the kids ready now. What's up?"

"I was thinking about joining you."

"What? You mean you aren't going to Holy Rock, your home away from home?"

"Nope. I'm sure Khalil and Xavier have things under control. And now that Stiles Graham is back, my presence won't be needed as much, so with that being said it's time I take advantage of these days of freedom, you know."

Fancy had mixed feelings about Khalil asking her to spend more time away from Holy Rock. Holy Rock was part of her life, of who she was, but like anything else in life, change happens and she had to adjust to it.

"That's great. And Victoria is coming, too. This is going to be fun. A real girl's day out.

"Victoria is off work?"

"Yeah, today and tomorrow. She said she had some days she had to take or she would lose them."

"Okay, then I'm glad I called."

"So am I. I should be on my way in about half an hour. I'll see you soon."

"Okay, by girl." Fancy ended the call and sauntered over to her immaculate walk-in closet with everything in its rightful place. The custom-made shelving made it easy for her to keep her clothes and shoes sorted. After settling on a pair of pink kaleidoscope printed leggings and a matching top, she picked out a pair of sneakers.

She put on her clothes and pulled her natural locs up in a bun on top of her head. Singing out loud, she sang, *"That's who you are... and I'm loved by you..."* one of her favorite songs by Chris Tomlin.

In the kitchen she made some toast and ate a grapefruit, foregoing her usual cup of coffee. Once she finished her light breakfast, she got her 32-ounce tumbler and filled it with spring water before grabbing her gym bag and heading out the door.

9

"Loyalty means I am down with you whether you are wrong or right. But I will tell you, when you are wrong and help you get it right." Unknown

Working out with Victoria and Tara proved to be just what Fancy needed. After their workout, they sat in the lounge of the Y talking.

"How's it going with that handsome hunk you're seeing?" Tara asked Fancy.

"I'm meeting him for lunch at one. So that should tell you a thing or two."

"I want to hear the down and dirty stuff."

"Victoria, girl, stop it," Fancy replied, laughing along with Tara.

"I have to agree with Victoria on this one, Fancy. I want to hear too."

"So, come on, tell us. What's going on with you two, girl?"

The ladies giggled like teenagers as Fancy told them, "All I'm going to tell you is he's not lacking anything in that department."

"Ahhhh," Victoria screamed.

"Shush," Tara said, tapping Victoria on the hand. "Folks are going to hear us."

"Girl, look around. There's no one in here except those two old ladies over there, and they don't seem the least bit interested in what's going on over here."

"Well, since we're playing true confessions, tell me how things are going with you and

Minister Davis? I was expecting to see you accompany him to the dinner we gave Stiles last night."

"For your information, he *did* invite me to go with him, and I told him I would. But my mother called while I was at work. My dad had to be taken to the hospital so you know I had to go see about him. That meant driving to Jackson, Tennessee. I couldn't leave her to deal with it all alone. She was scared to death."

"Oh, my. Is he okay?" asked Fancy.

"Yeah, you didn't mention it when we talked this morning," Tara said.

"Yes, she thought he'd had a stroke, but when they ran tests they said it wasn't a stroke. His blood pressure had spiked. My mother says she thinks he's been adding salt to his food, which he's not supposed to do. But Dad is a salt lover so it's hard to control that. As soon as she turns her back, he reaches for that salt container. Anyway, they got his pressure down and sent him home. He's going to be okay this time. I mean my parents are relatively young, in their sixties, but he's had problems with his blood pressure since he was in his twenties."

"Well, thank God he's going to be okay," Fancy said.

"So, let's get back to you and Minister Davis."

"Yeah, let's hear it," Tara added.

"Okay, but it's not what you think. I mean, he's a good guy. If you're asking if we've been intimate, the answer is no. We've kissed one time and that's it. He's a kind man but at the end of the day, I know he's not the one."

"But why?" Tara asked.

"He just isn't. First off, he's much older than the men I'm used to dating. He's set in his ways, but the main thing is he's still lamenting over his dead wife, and I can't compete with the dead. Every time we talk or go out to dinner, or anywhere, he compares me to her, or he's taking me to places the two of them used to go. Our conversations always end up being about her. I told him we can be friends and friends only 'cause I can't compete with her. You know what he said?"

"What?" Fancy asked.

"He said, "'You sound just like my wife.'"

"What! Oh, my God!" said Fancy.

Tara and Fancy broke out in spontaneous laughter.

"Ugghhh, creepy," Tara said, "I understand now. Don't you, Fancy?"

"Yea, I do. Look, girl, don't worry, you'll find someone who's more your type. You wait and see. You're attractive. You're funny, you have a great figure and a wonderful personality to go along with all that."

"Why, thank you, Fancy."

"She's speaking the truth. You watch, the perfect man is coming your way."

The ladies laughed and joked until Tara excused herself. It was time for her to pick up the kids from the on-site child care center.

Fancy and Victoria talked while they waited for Tara to get her kids. When Tara appeared at the front of the Y, the three ladies walked to the door.

"I'm so glad we did this," Fancy told the ladies as they walked outside. "I haven't laughed this hard in a long time."

"Me neither. We have to do this more often," Victoria said.

"I know that's right," Tara agreed.

"We will," Fancy said. "Definitely. I'll see y'all at Bible study Wednesday night."

"Okay, bye," said Victoria.

"Buh-bye," said Tara.

Each of the ladies went in separate directions to their parked cars.

Fancy laughed practically all the way home every time she thought about Victoria and Tara. They had turned out to be really good friends who she enjoyed hanging out with. Whenever they were around, Fancy was guaranteed a good laugh.

Once she got back home she took another shower and then sat down in her family room and began reading a book she had started on a few nights ago. Her text notifier chimed.

"Hey, hru"

Fancy smiled when she saw the text from Stiles.

"Good. HRU? Things going ok today?"

"Getting back in the swing of things. Picked up my ride. Niiice."

"Good for you."

"Coming to the church today?"

"No. Is everything ok?"

"Oh yea. Just asking. Well, gotta go. Heading to another meeting. TTYL."

"Sure, call me later if you get a chance."

"Will do."

10

"You can't always go by actions because some people will ACT like they love you just to get what they want from you." Sonya Parker

*D*etria sat in the office she rarely, if ever, utilized. She was nervous, knowing she had betrayed Hezekiah by telling Khalil about the meeting with him and Winston. She talked to herself as she got up from her chair and paced across the travertine floor. Hezekiah had said he wanted nothing more to do with her after tonight.

"Why am I nervous then? He wants me out of his life and I *want* to be out of his life. I don't know why I ever got mixed up with him anyway." And whoever this Winston guy really is, she didn't know. She just met him, gave him the envelope Hezekiah told her to give him, and told him what Hezekiah told her to tell him. She had no solid proof, but she suspected the envelope contained money. That was how Hezekiah operated. He paid others to carry out his sleazy work.

Winston was a good looking guy so she was pleasantly surprised when she first saw him. Real easy on the eyes. Before Khalil, she probably would have, no she *knew* she would have, gotten Winston in her bed, but she didn't want any other man since meeting Khalil.

"I shouldn't care what Hezekiah thinks," she tried convincing herself. "As for Khalil, maybe this will show him he can trust me, that I have his back. Dee, you cannot afford for this to backfire in your face. It would destroy every hope you have of becoming First Lady McCoy." She stopped talking to herself when she heard the doorbell chiming.

She looked at the clock sitting on the sleek white desk. It was six-forty five. It had to be Hezekiah. She didn't think Winston would come forty five minutes early.

"Dee," she heard Priscilla call. "Deeetriuhh," she called out again.

Dee exhaled and then opened the door to the office and headed down the long hall leading to the front of the house. Sure enough, there sat Hezekiah in his wheelchair.

"You can come to the office. That's where we're meeting. Where's Benny?"

"He's gone. I told him I would call him when I'm ready. He's not far. He has customers out this way."

Priscilla gave Detria a look that told her she didn't agree with whatever Detria had going on now.

"Priscilla, I'm expecting someone else. When he comes will you show him to the office?"

Priscilla nodded. "Yes. Would you like something to drink, Reverend McCoy?"

"Thank you, Priscilla. I believe I would. Water with lemon and if you have any scotch, I'd like a shot, no ice."

"I'll bring it to you in the office. Anything to eat?"

Hezekiah raised a hand. "No, I've had dinner. Thank you, Priscilla."

"You're welcome." She turned and walked off while Detria and Hezekiah continued until they arrived to the open door of her office.

The spacious bright white Mediterranean office was inviting with a teal velvet sofa and large windows that allowed natural light to illuminate the space. A white fireplace was flanked by built-in bookshelves. An oversized piece of colorful art brought out the popping color of the sofa and complemented the vibrant teal blue tufted chairs.

Hezekiah was able to easily maneuver in the space without fear of bumping into anything.

Priscilla returned with his water and scotch just as the doorbell chimed again.

"That's probably our guest," Hezekiah said, looking at Detria.

"Priscilla," said Detria.

"I'll bring him back," Priscilla replied.

"Thanks, Priscilla."

Moments later, Khalil entered the room much to Hezekiah's amazement. An immediate scowl formed over his face. "What the hell are you doing here?" he barked.

Khalil replied with a wicked smile. "Hi, Father. I'm delighted to see you too."

Hezekiah glared at Detria. "Did you know about this?"

A lump formed in Dee's throat. Before she could answer, Priscilla ushered in Winston.

"Good even—" Winston stopped in mid-sentence when he entered the office next and saw Khalil in the room. He deflected his eyes from Dee to Khalil to the man he assumed was Hezekiah McCoy. He'd never laid physical eyes on Hezekiah, but he knew it was him because the man was sitting in a wheelchair, and he and Khalil highly favored each other. "Good evening," he finished his sentence. "Ah, what's going on here?"

"I'd liked the answer to that question myself," seethed Hezekiah.

"And so would I," Khalil retorted. "But it looks like you and my father have plotted against my mother. And I don't like what I'm seeing."

Detria remained quiet, cowering lip in the corner of the room near the fireplace.

"You know my father and you're smashing my mom?" Khalil walked up on Winston and stood in his face, toe-to-toe.

"I don't know your father."

"You're a liar. Why are you here then?"

"Detria contacted me, told me your father wanted to see me." Winston was by no means scared, but he wanted to restrain himself from knocking out the young man standing in his face. Out of respect for his mother was the only reason he didn't punch his lights out. As for Hezekiah, he didn't know what kind of game this man was playing, but it wasn't worth Winston getting into a brawl or something worse because of it, especially if it was over a woman.

"I guess I should be asking you why I'm here," Winston turned, walked a step back from Khalil and focused his stare on Hezekiah.

Hezekiah, biting on his bottom lip, looked at Detria like he could kill her right on the spot.

"Well, seems like since you, my darling, arranged for us all to be here, I guess there's no reason to hide my hand. Detria works for me. She has for quite some time. I should say she's worked for me and in return I make sure she's supplied with all the powder and any other drug she wants."

If Detria could have made herself disappear, she would have rather than face Khalil's hardened stare.

"So this is how you do it?" His features twisted into a maddening sneer.

"No, Khalil. That's not true. Don't listen to him." She gave him a quick, denying glance.

"If you're doing my father's dirty deeds in return for drugs you've reached an all-time low. You're nothing but trash. I always knew you were. I'm glad I took you for every dime I could."

Detria broke out crying. "Please, Khalil." She ran over to him and reached out for him but he pushed her away, causing her to fall to the floor.

"Hold up, man. No need for all of that. She's a lady." Winston spoke up, walked over to where Detria was and reached down his hand to help her off the floor.

"Hah, lady? I don't think so," Khalil spewed.

Without knocking, Priscilla entered the room. "Excuse me, can I get any of you anything?"

"No! Just leave, Priscilla. Get out," screamed Detria.

Priscilla abruptly turned, slammed the office door shut, and left.

"You want to know why he's here? You think I don't know he's smashing your mother? You think he just happened to meet her by accident?

Then ask him? Ask him how much I just paid him to keep seeing your mother. Go on, ask him."

Khalil's nostrils flared. You could see his arteries throbbing in his neck. He balled his fists and took three giant steps forward toward his father. Without holding back, he hit Hezekiah in his face.

Blood gushed from Hezekiah's mouth and nose.

"Stop it! Stop it, Khalil," Detria screamed with a thread of hysteria in her voice.

Hezekiah used one hand to wipe the blood from his face.

Winston, though furious with what Hezekiah said, pulled Khalil back and away from his father.

Hezekiah, undetected, texted Benny. "Come now. Trouble."

Khalil jerked away from Winston. "Don't you ever step foot in my mother's house again. If I even hear of you coming near her, I swear I'll kill you."

Hezekiah laughed and then looked up at his son. A glower spread over his face as his bloody mouth began to swell. "That's my boy. A real chip off the old block." Hezekiah continued to taunt his son while Detria sat in the chair crying like a baby and Winston turned to go out of the office.

"Hey, you. You heard my boy. But thanks for everything. Keep the five grand I gave you for making it good for the First Lady."

Khalil ran to his father again with balled fists. "I'd think twice about that if I were you," Benny said as he walked into the office. "You okay?" He removed his glasses and revealed hard, gelatin eyes.

"Never better," Hezekiah shot back. "Get me out of here."

Fancy was distraught after Khalil rushed to her house after leaving Detria's. He told her everything that had transpired.

"But I...how...how could Winston do this? I thought we had something special. And your father, why does he want to keep hurting me?" She cried so hard she began hyperventilating.

Khalil gathered her in his arms and pulled her next to him as they sat on her sofa. "I'm sorry, Ma. But it's better you found out now than on down the road. The man is filth. I told him never to set foot in this house again. If he does, let me know."

"I can't believe this. There has to be some explanation. There just has to be."

Xavier stormed into his mother's house. Khalil called him after leaving Detria's house and told him everything that had gone down.

"Ma, are you okay?" he asked, running and sitting down on the other side of her.

Fancy continued crying. "Why? *Whyyy?*"

Khalil and Xavier looked up at each other. The unspoken words of the two brothers was written all over their faces. They had to protect their mother by any means necessary.

While they were consoling their mother, her cell phone rang.

Xavier got up and walked over to where the phone lay on the foyer table. "It's him," he said, looking at Khalil.

Khalil jumped up from the sofa.

"Don't answer it," Fancy begged. "Just leave it alone."

"Didn't I tell you not to contact my mother?"

"I need to talk to her. I need to explain. Where is she?"

"You don't need to explain a darn thing. It's clear what you were after. You're nothing but a paid gigolo. You stay away from her. I'm warning you." Khalil ended the call and Fancy ran off to her bedroom in tears, slamming the door behind her.

"Ma...Ma." Xavier followed and knocked on his mother's bedroom door. He could hear her crying.

Khalil walked up and called her name too.

"Ma, can we come in?"

"Just leave. I can't talk right now."

"Ma, please," Xavier implored.

"Ma, we just want to make sure you're okay and then I promise, we'll leave," Khalil explained.

Fancy sat up and moved to the edge of the bed. "Come in."

Xavier opened the door. He saw his mother sitting on the end of her bed, her eyes beet red and her hands trembling. He walked over to her and knelt beside her.

"Ma, don't cry. Please don't cry."

"I'm sorry this happened," Khalil said as he came up and stood beside his brother. "I wish things could have been different for you. You deserve the best of everything, and I'm sorry our father did you this way. I'm sorry that punk hurt you, too."

"Ma, it's going to be a'ite. You'll see," Xavier reassured her.

"I... I just need to be alone right now. Please, the two of you should go home."

"But we don't want to leave you like this," Xavier pleaded.

"I told you, I'm good."

"I'll stay the night," Khalil offered.

"No, please, I'm fine. Just go. I need time to sort everything out. I promise I'll be all right."

Xavier got off of his knees and stood next to Khalil.

"Okay, we'll go, but if dude comes over here, do not let him in, Ma. Please."

"I won't. Now just go." She shooed them away and stood. Walking out of her room, she paused, looked at them, and tilted her head to the side slightly and continued walking.

Khalil and Xavier followed her as she led them to the door.

"Are you sure you're going to be okay here by yourself?"

"Xavier, honey, yes."

Each of them kissed her on the cheek and then walked out of the door.

Fancy closed and locked the door behind them. Returning to her room, she lay back down again on her bed and allowed her tears to freely fall.

The ringing of her phone continued for some time as Winston kept calling. She only answered it when Khalil called to check on her and shortly thereafter Xavier texted her. She responded by assuring both of them she was fine but she and God knew better.

When she heard the doorbell, she looked at her phone and saw Winston outside her door. She lived in a gated community but there were times cars trailed closely behind another car when the gate opened. That way they were able to gain entrance into Lion's Gate without buzzing the resident. As a measure of added security, she was glad she'd listened to Khalil's advice and gotten a doorbell camera installed. She watched as he continued to press the doorbell and nervously rock from side to side. How dare he come to her home after what he'd done. She wanted nothing to do with him.

Her phone rang but again she refused to answer. After ringing the doorbell and pounding on her door for several minutes, he finally turned and left.

The hurt she felt turned to rage as she thought of how low down and dirty Hezekiah had been. She called the last number he'd called her from. Much to her surprise, he answered.

"Hi, Fancy, to what do I owe this call?"

"How could you? And why would you want to hurt me, Hezekiah? What happened to the man I fell in love with?"

"I guess he went wherever the woman I felt in love with went. And how can you call me and talk about hurt? You and my sons have done everything you possibly can to destroy me. My son stole over a hundred thousand dollars of my money. And you, you're behind this whole charge that's been brought against me. You know what prison is like, Fancy, yet, you want to send me back there?"

"You are the one who embezzled from Holy Rock, Hezekiah, not me. I never wanted to see you go back to prison, but this is your doing. I can't believe you would hire someone to do what Winston did to me."

"You've always been so naïve, so vulnerable. Stop the crying. Act like a grown woman instead of a stupid, silly high school girl. If you like him so much, call him up. I'm sure he'll be willing to come back."

"Why, you sick son of..."she mouthed, followed by a stream of expletives.

"Now, now, Fancy, I don't think that kind of talk is very First lady like. Remember what I told you, you reap what you sow. But, just so you know, I'm not done. Khalil stole from me and he's going to get what's coming to him, too. Now, if you'll excuse me, I'm sick of hearing your pathetic self on this phone. Goodnight, love." Hezekiah ended the call.

Fancy crawled underneath the bed covers and cried herself to sleep.

11

"Once you've been hurt, it is so hard to get attached again. The fear that it will happen again is what builds the walls around your heart.
Unknown

*T*he days passed in slow motion. Fancy spent most of her time secluded in her house away from family, away from Holy Rock, and avoiding phone calls. Victoria and Tara would not give up trying to reach her. Not knowing what had happened since the last time they were together at the Y, the ladies were quite concerned, especially when she didn't show up for mid-week or Sunday's services.

Victoria sent her a lengthy text message for the millionth time. "Fancy, plz tell me what's going on. Tara and I have been calling and texting but you don't answer. You weren't at midweek service or Sunday. Pastor Khalil says you're taking some time to yourself, but he encouraged us to reach out to you. That tells me something isn't right. It's not like you not to respond to me or Tara. No matter what's going on, we're ur friends. If it's something Winston or your ex have done, we can help you get past it. Please answer me."

Fancy cried again as she read Victoria's text but she didn't reply to it. Victoria and Tara meant well. She knew they did, but she was out of energy, and drained spiritually and emotionally. She read the text over again. Maybe she did need someone to talk to other than Khalil and Xavier. She hadn't even talked to Stiles, not that he'd called. He was supposed to be returning to Texas the following day, so knowing him like she did, she figured he would call to tell her goodbye before leaving. But the space she was in now, she couldn't care less if he called to say goodbye or not.

Winston continued to call and text until Fancy had enough and blocked him. There was absolutely nothing he could say or do to excuse what he'd done. Just the knowledge alone that he'd conspired with Hezekiah for God knows what reason was enough to be done with him. The only reason she could come up with for Hezekiah to pay him to get to know her and her sons was because of his arrest. He also had said something about Khalil having stolen money from him. What could he have been talking about?

Fancy called Khalil. "Ma, hey, how you feeling this morning?"

"I'm okay. I wanted to ask you something."

"Go for it."

"Hezekiah said you stole money from him—a hundred thousand dollars to be exact. What's he talking about, Khalil?"

Khalil cleared his throat. "I have no idea, Ma. Dude is so full of it. I mean, he's such a liar. What money could I have stolen from him? Guess he's talking about the fact we busted his behind. And now I'm the one running Holy Rock. He hates that."

Fancy listened. "Yeah, I'm sure you're right. I've been trying to sort things out in my brain. Everything that happened last week has been rough on me. I can't tell you how betrayed, how violated, and used I feel."

"Ma, that's why me and Xavier told you to do something to get your mind off my father and off that Winston fellow. Why don't you go out of town for a few days. I bet Victoria would go with you. You're always saying she likes to travel."

"I'm not in the mindset to travel, Khalil. Anyway, I'll talk to you later."

"Ma, wait. Why don't I come by and pick you up for lunch this afternoon. Stiles is leaving tomorrow and we're going to go to that spot downtown that just opened. The food is supposed to be super good." He couldn't believe he was inviting her to be in Stiles' company, but things were different. His mother needed a deterrent. Stiles was just the guy to hopefully make her forget her problems for at least a couple hours or so.

"No, I don't think so, but tell him I said to have a safe trip. I'll talk to you later, son. Bye." She ended the call and then followed up with a call to Victoria.

"Fancy, God, I'm so glad to finally hear from you. Tara and I have been worried sick about you, girl. What's going on?"

"I can't begin to tell you everything over the phone, Vic."

"I'm getting off at one o'clock today. Do you want me to come over? I'll call Tara to see if she can come or it can just be me and you. Whatever you'd like."

"Ok, but just you, if you don't mind. Tara would have to bring the baby, which I wouldn't mind in any other circumstances, but not today. My mind can't handle it."

"Fancy, you have me worried. Okay, anyway, I should be there around one thirty. Do you want me to stop and bring you something to eat? Or get a bottle of wine."

"Nah, I don't think so."

"I'll call you before I come and then you can let me know if you've changed your mind and want me to grab something."

"Thanks, Victoria. I will. Bye now."

Fancy exhaled slightly, feeling relieved that she'd reached out to Victoria. She went into the kitchen and poured herself something to drink. She hadn't had much of an appetite.

"About to head ur way. stopping at the sub shop to get me a black bean burger. Want anything?"

"I guess you can bring me one with all the trimmings."

"Anything else? Wine? Soda?"

"No. I have wine and soda here."

"Okay, got it. Be there as soon as I can."

Victoria arrived less than an hour after texting Fancy. The ladies sat outside on the patio. The weather was perfect for an end of summer day.

Victoria helped herself in Fancy's kitchen and retrieved two glasses from the cabinet and filled them with some iced tea Fancy said she had in the refrigerator.

"Here you go." Victoria walked out onto the patio and placed the glasses on the table. After that, she returned to the kitchen and brought back two plates to put their sandwiches on.

I got us potato chips too."

"What's my bill?" Fancy asked.

"Girl, please. I got it." Victoria proceeded to sit down and then opened the bags of food, passing Fancy's over to her.

"Thanks, Vic."

"Now tell me what's going on with you. I know it has to be serious for you not to come to church or call or text me and Tara back. And when Pastor Khalil told us you needed a friend, we knew we had to do something. Girl, I was ready to bust through those gates out there."

"You're crazy, Vic."

"I'm for real."

Once Fancy started talking she couldn't stop until she shared every detail with Victoria.

Victoria listened intently without saying a word until Fancy was done. She reached across the patio table and held her friend's hand. "I'm so so sorry. I can't believe all of this happened and you're just telling me. How could Hezekiah be so low down? And Winston? Wow, we thought he was the cat's meow and he turned out to be a snake. This sounds too unreal, Fancy."

"Yeah, tell me about it." Fancy wiped a tear from her eye.

"I don't know what to say."

"It's okay. I'm just glad I got it out. Thank you for listening and for being my friend, Victoria. I know I should have told you…and Tara too, but I've been trying to find a way to deal with this."

"Yeah, but you don't need to deal with it alone. All I can say is God will make a way. I know this might not help much, but I'm glad he revealed Winston's real intentions. As for Pastor McCoy, he's just mad because of the divorce and because he's facing some serious prison time. But none of that is your fault. He's the one who forced you out of your home, turned his back on you and the boys, and was stealing from Holy Rock. He only has himself to blame. And for him to do you like he did, girl, you better believe his day is coming. He's really gone too far. God don't like ugly, but I shouldn't have to tell you that."

"Yea. It just hurts so bad, Victoria." Fancy began crying.

Victoria got up and walked around to where Fancy was seated. She leaned in and wrapped her arms around her friend. "It's going to be okay. You're going to come out of this on top. You watch what I tell you. You'll see. God's got you." Releasing her from the hug, Fancy looked up and then squeezed Victoria's hand.

"Now, what do you say we open that bottle of Moscato I saw in your fridge? We need to toast to better days ahead."

Fancy picked up a napkin off the table and wiped her tears and blew her snotty nose.

"Ugh," Victoria said and laughed.

Fancy laughed too. She got up and followed Victoria as they went into the kitchen.

12

Khalil and Stiles talked over lunch about
when he would next return to Holy Rock. "So it's
all good, you're coming back for your installation
as associate pastor the second Sunday in
September, right?"

"Yes, and I plan to bring some of the
members of Full of Grace with me."

"Cool. Let me know how many will be coming.
I can arrange for hotel discounts or find suitable
places for them to stay. Whatever it takes."

"I appreciate that."

Khalil continued enjoying his salmon burger
and fries while Stiles dined on a huge mock
chicken salad sandwich and fries.

"Have you heard from my brother?"

"No, not really," Khalil replied.

"Do you have his contact information? The
number I have always goes straight to an
automated voicemail message. You know that
mechanical voice that answers when your phone
is turned off."

"I'll give you the number I have in my
Contacts, but I can't promise you it works. It
may be the same number you have."

"I don't know what else to do. He doesn't want anything to do with me. That's evident by his lack of response or reaching out to me."

"All I can say to that is to leave him alone. If he doesn't want to get to know you as his brother, and he can't forgive his father, then turn him over to God. That's what I've done. I can't be bothered about him. You know?"

"Yea. Well, how is Fancy? I didn't see her at midweek service or at any of the Sunday services last week? Did I miss her? I know that's easy to do with the massive congregation you have. It's easy to get lost in the crowd."

"No, you didn't miss her. She wasn't there, but she's good. She's just taking some much needed time away."

"That's understandable. I'll give her a call later this evening or tomorrow before I get out of here."

Khalil didn't respond. Instead he took another bite of his food. "Excuse me," he said when his cell phone rang. "Yes, Eliana."

"Hi, Khalil...uh, there's someone here to see you."

"Did I miss an appointment or counseling session? I don't have it on my calendar and you didn't say anything about me having an appointment when I left."

"No, it's...it's your father."

"I'm on the way." Khalil ended the call, wiped his mouth, then opened his wallet and pulled out two twenty dollar bills and one ten.

Stiles saw the strange look that suddenly appeared on Khalil's face and heard the concern in his voice. "Everything straight?"

"Nah, we need to get back to Holy Rock. I think you just talked up the devil."

Eliana explained to Hezekiah that Khalil was not in the office. Hezekiah insisted she call Khalil and let him know he was at Holy Rock.

"I'm sure he'll want to head back if you'll call and tell him I'm here, Sista."

Hezekiah wanted to show his son that he wasn't the only one who could show up uninvited and unannounced. It was time out for hiding his hand. Hezekiah wanted what was his, and intended to get it at all costs.

"Pastor McCoy, Lord have mercy, it sure is good to see you," Sista Mavis jumped up out of her chair, rushed out of her work space, and dashed toward Hezekiah when she saw him at Eliana's desk.

"Sista Mavis, God bless you. Don't you look good." Hezekiah reached out toward her and she stepped into his arms for a hug.

Sista Mavis blushed. "Thank you, Pastor McCoy. God's been good to me. Looks like he's been good to you too. You're looking mighty spiffy. And sounding good too."

"Yes, the Lord has been good to me. Like the words to that old spiritual, I won't complain."

Several other staff members came out of their offices and work spaces to greet Hezekiah, making him feel good that he had been missed.

"I'll see if I can reach Pastor Khalil."

"Thank you. God bless you, young lady."

"If you'll excuse me. I'll be right back." Eliana got up, went to Khalil's office, and called to tell him what was going on.

Hezekiah watched Eliana as she walked up the hall. *Dang, she fine. I bet my son is tappin' that. If he ain't, he's crazy.*

When Eliana returned, Hezekiah was still standing around her desk talking to Sista Mavis and two of the ministers and one of the other admin assistants.

Eliana looked at Sista Mavis as she lingered around Eliana's desk.

"Did you reach him? Is he at lunch?"

"Yes, sir, I was able to get in touch with him. He's on his way back. He should be here in about twenty or thirty minutes."

"Sounds good."

Hezekiah turned and continued listening to the others gathered around him. However, Sista Mavis was overpowering most of them, trying to dig for information in Sista Mavis fashion.

Hezekiah knew Sista Mavis like the back of his hand.

"Excuse me, Pastor McCoy, when you're done talking I'll show you to the small conference room. You can wait on Pastor Khalil in there if you'd like."

"That'll be fine. And I'm sure Sista Mavis wouldn't mind taking me there. Would you, Sista Mavis?" Hezekiah flashed a smile at Sista Mavis and grabbed her hand.

"Now, Pastor you know you don't have to ask me that. Of course I'll take you." She turned and looked at Eliana.

"Eliana, you just go on with your day. I'll take care of Pastor McCoy. You know I used to be his assistant."

"Yes, I know. But really, I don't mind, Pastor McCoy. I know Sista Mavis has a lot on her plate."

"No, no, no. I have plenty of time to finish doing what I was doing," Sista Mavis insisted and stood next to Hezekiah's chair.

"Thank you, Sista Mavis," Hezekiah said.

"Would you like some water, coffee, a soda? I can go get you something to eat from the kitchen if you'd like."

Hezekiah showed both palms. "No, I'm good. You were always good at taking care of me, Sista Mavis. I see you haven't changed."

Sista Mavis blushed again and then looked over at Eliana and rolled her eyes in self-satisfaction "Well, if you're ready, I'll show you to the conference room, Pastor."

"Wait, Sista Mavis, the conference room is locked. You'll need the key," Eliana reminded her.

"Oh, yea, I guess we will need that won't we, Pastor?" Sista Mavis chuckled.

Eliana retrieved the key from her desk and passed it to Sista Mavis.

"Thank you, child."

"You're welcome, and if you need anything, Pastor McCoy, just let me know. There's a phone in there that calls directly to my desk."

"And mine, too," added Sista Mavis.

"Thank you, young lady. Now, Sista Mavis, what do you say I lead the way," Hezekiah said, "unless it's moved. It does look different around here."

"Yes, there's been quite a bit of remodeling but the small conference room is still in the same place."

Hezekiah pointed. "Up that hallway and to the left?"

"That's right," answered Sista Mavis.

"Is First Lady Fancy in her office today?" he asked Sista Mavis as they made the trek to the conference room.

"No, she hasn't been here in a coupla weeks. She missed midweek service and Sunday services last week, too. That was unusual. She used to be here every time these doors opened. You didn't hear it from me, but I'm telling you things just haven't been the same since you've been gone, Pastor. I don't think your sons want her here as much. And you know, Pastor Stiles came back."

"Oh, is that right?"

"Yes, he's the associate pastor. He hasn't moved back to Memphis permanently yet. But I suspect he will soon."

"Interesting."

"Pastor, I don't mean to be disrespectful, but I'm just saying, you're the last person I'd expect to pop up at Holy Rock."

"Why is that, Sista Mavis?"

"It's no secret that your sons and Sista McCoy don't have the best feelings for you. You know what I mean? And it was all on the news about your arrest. I'm sorry, I shouldn't have mentioned that." She looked around like she was checking to see if anyone was in earshot.

"No worries, Sista Mavis. I've tried to make amends with my family even though they turned their backs on me when I had my stroke. It almost destroyed me. It's no wonder I didn't have another stroke after that. But God." Hezekiah's facial expression changed to one of dismay.

"Lord, that's a shame. I can't understand that but thank God the good Lord took care of you. When your friends and family forsake you, He's with you."

"Thank you for saying that, Sista Mavis. It's important to me that you know, Sista Mavis, the allegations about me embezzling money are all lies spearheaded by them, too. But I still love my family—unconditionally and I forgive them. If I didn't then you and I know the good Lord won't forgive me for my wrong doing."

Sista Mavis shook her head. "I know you love your family, Pastor. You always have. You gave that woman and those sons of yours any and everything they wanted. And just so you know, I don't believe you stole from this church. You love Holy Rock too much to do anything like that."

They arrived at the conference room. Sista Mavis pulled the key out of her pocket and unlocked the door. "But you're on the mend now. God's going to restore everything the enemy stole from you. He's going to give you double for your trouble."

"Thank you, Sista Mavis. I believe that. In spite of what they've done and what they're still trying to do to ruin my life, I want to be in their lives. That's why I'm here today. Neither of my sons will take my phone calls. I haven't seen them since my divorce was finalized. And even then, they didn't say a word to me at the courthouse. I've prayed and I've prayed. First God told me I needed to remain still—until now. He told me to come to Holy Rock. He told me I have to be the bigger person. That I'm the head and it's up to me to try to work this out."

Sista Mavis sat in the chair and began shaking her head. "Lord, how terrible."

"If they still don't want anything to do with me after today, then I'll just have to go on about my way. Wash my hands, you know. But, honestly, I miss this place, Sista Mavis. I miss you and the people at Holy Rock."

"Pastor, you're a good man. Always have been, but you know these young folks. You can't tell them a thing these days. I'm telling you, we're living in the last days."

"Let me ask you something, Sista Mavis."

"What is it, Pastor McCoy?"

"Is my baby boy around?"

"I haven't seen him all morning. Sometimes he doesn't come in until the afternoon. I can check for you. His office is right pass here."

"If you'll check for me, I would appreciate it."

"Yes, sir. Just stay right here and let me go see."

Sista Mavis left out of the conference room and closed the door behind her.

Hezekiah gloated. He still had an ally in Sista Mavis. He needed someone he could trust and manipulate at Holy Rock. Listening to her proved she would be perfect. She'd already told him more than he knew. To hear that Fancy hadn't been in the office in over a week put a smile on his face. *I bet she's somewhere bawling her pretty little eyes out.*

Sista Mavis returned shortly after she left. "He's not in his office. I checked with Sista Eliana. She said he was out of the office today attending a youth seminar at the convention center."

"Oh, okay. Thank you for checking."

The phone in the conference room rang. Sista Mavis walked over to the opposite end of the twelve-seat conference table where the phone was located. "Hello."

"Sista Mavis, Minister Davis needs to see you."

"Ok, thank you. Tell him I'm on my way." Sista Mavis looked at Hezekiah.

"It's all right. I didn't mean to keep you away from work, Sista Mavis. You've been more than helpful."

"You just call me if you need me, Pastor McCoy. God bless you. And I'm praying that you'll be back in the pulpit real soon. God can do it, you know?"

"Yes, He sure can. I'll see you before I leave."

Sista Mavis left the conference room, leaving Hezekiah in a much better frame of mind than when he first came through the doors of Holy Rock. He looked at the walls. His picture was still hanging on the wall, along with a picture of his bastard brother, Stiles Graham, and his no-good father, Pastor Chauncey Graham. Added to the wall of past preachers was a picture of his son, Khalil.

He pulled out his cell phone to call Benny to let him know it would be a while before he came out. Benny assured him he was still parked outside and would wait on him for however long it took.

Almost as quickly as he ended the call with Benny, the conference room door flew open. In walked Khalil. Behind him was Stiles.

"So, Father, what do I owe this pleasure?" Stiles closed the door behind them.

"*Sooo*, tell me li'l brother, how much of my money did my son pay you to come back to Holy Rock as his crony?"

"Hello, to you, too," replied Stiles.

"I asked you a question. Now what do you want?" Khalil said in a raised voice, and interloping his arms and taking a hard stance while he stared down at his father.

"You sure you want to talk about this in front of him?" Hezekiah looked past Khalil and over at Stiles.

"I'll step out."

"No, no need. There's nothing this fool has to say that you can't hear. What do you want?"

"I want the 100 grand you stole from me. I'm running out of patience, son."

Stiles looked at Khalil, his eyes bucked.

"You must be abusing those drugs they gave you when you had that stroke. I don't know what you're talking about."

"You should know that I'm not one to be messed with."

"Oh, are you going to send those goons back to try and rob and kill me?"

"What is he talking about, Hezekiah? You tried to kill your own son? Man, nothing can be that serious. What's wrong with you?"

"You stay out of this, Stiles," barked Hezekiah.

"Is that what you're going to do? You hurt my mother, you hurt her real bad, and I'm going to do everything in my power to make you and that Winston fellow pay for what you did."

"Your mother is a strong woman. If you don't know that by now, that's on you. She should be the last person you're worried about."

"And if I were you, I'd be spending my last days of freedom trying to right your wrongs instead of trying to dig a grave for me. You're a pathetic weakling. And to think, I used to look up to you, respect you. I thought you meant what you said when you stood behind that pulpit Sunday after Sunday, week after week. But you're nothing but a charlatan. A thief. A liar. I can't wait until you're back behind bars."

Hezekiah released a loud, resounding laugh. "You think those trumped up charges of yours are going to stick? You have no solid proof that I've embezzled a dime from this church. And you," Hezekiah looked at Stiles, "you're back here at Holy Rock, you better try to teach this boy a thing or two or he's going to find himself back on the streets hustling drugs and knocking old ladies in the head. Now, I'm telling you one last time, I want my money, Khalil."

"And I'm telling you to get out of my church and don't ever come back. And if I ever find out that you or that Winston fellow, or any of your cronies come near my mother again or even so much as dial her number, you're the one who's going to be sorry."

"Stop it. This isn't right," Stiles spoke up. "Look, I don't know about this money you say Khalil stole from you. I don't know if you, Hezekiah, embezzled money from Holy Rock. I know nothing about any of it, but I do know one thing, we're supposed to be men of God. How can all this discord be happening? What happened to you, Hezekiah to make you so bitter? And you, Khalil, you're up in the pulpit every Sunday preaching the Word, why do you have so much hatred toward your father? Hezekiah, ever since I found out you were my biological brother, I've tried to reach out to you. Tried to have a relationship with you, but for some reason you won't acknowledge me or have anything to do with me. You're in God's house talking about killing your own son. And I don't know what you've done to Fancy, but none of this is acceptable to God."

"Don't preach to me. You can't tell me a thing. Look at your own track record. Your first wife would rather be with another woman than be with you. And your second wife is maim and crippled all because of you and your failure to be a husband to her. Your kid is dead, your sister is dead, her husband is dead, and that poor excuse of a father is nothing but a lying wolf all dressed up in sheep's clothing. So get the heck out of my face with your foolery."

Stiles was beside himself with anger. Hezekiah's words had been biting, to the point Stiles wanted to beat Hezekiah to a pulp, but he restrained himself. Just as quickly as he'd spoken about God and being right, he'd quickly tossed his words out of the window after hearing his brother's vicious verbal attack.

"Get out of here. Now," Khalil yelled or I'll call security and get them to throw your sorry behind out."

"Do what you will but let this serve as your last warning. Get me my money. Every single penny of it that you stole from my condo."

Khalil flung the door open and stood to the side.

Hezekiah pushed the ON button of his power chair and maneuvered himself out of the room and into the hall. He looked over his shoulder as he neared the front where Eliana, Sista Mavis, and the rest of the admins and the receptionist sat. "I want my money, Khalil," he barked.

Sista Mavis looked up when she heard the loud yelling and talking. Eliana and the others did too.

"Let me out of here," Hezekiah said as he approached the door.

Khalil and Stiles stood just out of view of the office staff.

Hezekiah had crossed the line too many times. Khalil had to step up his game. How? He didn't know just yet. Maybe Stiles returning to Memphis was a good thing. Or maybe it was time Khalil returned to what was familiar—the streets-to get things done.

13

"There's no place like home, there's no place like home." John Howard Payne

"I'm beginning to understand why God had me to accept the position at Holy Rock."

"What do you mean exactly?" Kareena asked as they drove away from George Bush Intercontinental Airport.

"First, let me tell you I was treated like a king. My crib is straight, got a smooth ride at my disposal, neither of which I have to pay a dime for and then a salary that won't have me stressing about a thing. God is good, Kareena."

"I'm glad to hear that. But is that what you meant by you understand now why God sent you back there?"

"Not exactly. I see my family needs me. My presence at Holy Rock is needed. There's a lot going on. Family dissension. Father pitted against sons. Husband against wife. Brother against brother. It's a mess, Kareena, and I found myself in the middle of it yesterday, the day before leaving to come back home. I guess God has his reasons for not letting me witness how bad the dysfunction was in the family until yesterday."

"Is there anything you can do to help? And why are your nephews against each other?"

"Oh, I wasn't talking about Khalil and Xavier against one another, although I do know Khalil can't get pass the fact Xavier is gay. I was talking about me and my brother. Hezekiah came to Holy Rock yesterday. Unannounced of course. He made some serious accusations and even more serious threats toward Khalil. The enemy is definitely out for blood is all I can say. I'm glad to be back in Houston, but I'm still carrying that scene that unfolded yesterday with me. It's in my mind and I can't get it out. I've got to do some serious praying. I need to hear clearly from God about what I need to do."

Kareena listened with her whole heart. Whatever went down in Memphis had Stiles upset and worried. His family must have really shown out some kind of way.

"Enough about me and my family. How have things been here?"

"You and I have talked almost every day, so you know things at Full of Grace are good. Reverend Givens stepped up and showed out in your absence. He may have just joined the Full of Grace staff but he would have made you proud. Were you able to look at the livestream?"

"No, unfortunately not. I was in church service the same time our services were being streamed. Did you make a tape I can go back and watch?"

"You know I did. It's in your office."

"Anybody join?"

"Yes, we had two people to join last Sunday."

"Good. I'm glad to hear that. At least I don't have to come back to a lot of drama."

"Are you hungry? Do you need to stop and get something to eat?"

"No, I'm good. I'll get out and get something later if I need to. You can just take me home and I'll get my car. I need to go to Full of Grace."

"You don't have to do that unless you just want to. I can take you. I was going back there anyway. I have a few things I need to finish up. I really don't mind."

"I might be there awhile. I mean it's already going on three o'clock. You're usually out of there by five."

"I don't mind staying later if you need me to. There's always something for me to work on, and you might need me to go over some of the things I put on your desk for your review."

"What about your fiancé? I don't want River to feel as if I'm embarking on his time." Stiles fished.

"River is out of town on business, so I don't have any plans for this evening. Plus, he understands how much time my job involves. He's good with that. He's a busy man himself."

"Okay, in that case, let's stop by Carl's Jr. I've been wanting to try that new vegan burger combo they have. They don't have a Carl's Jr. in Memphis. We can take it back to the church, unless you want to dine out somewhere."

"No, I'll get me something from Carl's. That'll be my dinner."

"Great, Carl's Jr. it is."

Sitting in the conference room attached to Stiles' office, he and Kareena ate and talked.

She pressed him to talk about what had gone on in Memphis.

"How was your father?"

"I would be lying if I said I'm not concerned about him. Physically, he's getting around as good as I am, but mentally he's getting confused. Poor Josie, she's worried sick about him. I don't blame her. The neurologist has him on some medicine that's supposed to help slow the progression of the disease."

"So he has Alzheimer's?"

"Dementia. Josie is changing his diet, taking him off meat and sticking more to a plant-based diet. Research shows that a plant-based diet may help people with dementia and Alzheimer's."

"That's good to know. I'll keep praying for him. And I'm sorry to hear so much discord is going on within your family. I was hoping you would be able to connect with your brother while you were there. Maybe all is not lost. You'll be going back and forth to Memphis so things stand a chance of getting better."

"Yep. Nothing is impossible with God. I think my brother just has a lot of pride. Plus, he's hurt. I can't say I blame him. I mean it was tough for me learning the woman I thought was my mother wasn't my biological mother, but instead she was my aunt. So I guess I understand some of what's going on inside his head. He has a lot of bitterness built up. He believes Pastor knew about him all along but made no effort when he was a kid to see him or get to know him. But our biological mother had serious mental issues. I don't know how much of that is true. All I do know is at some point we have to forgive and try to move forward."

Kareena gave him a hard stare. Here he was talking about forgiving and moving forward in life yet he couldn't let go of his own past. He couldn't seem to truly forgive those who had hurt his heart.

"Did you just hear yourself?"

"What?"

"You're talking about forgiving, but have you forgiven yourself and others who hurt *you*? You won't even allow yourself to love. How is that forgiving?"

"Look, you and I both know that's not my problem. I believe I can say that I *have* forgiven myself and I've forgiven the ones that hurt me. If you're talking about me and you, the timing just wasn't right, Kareena. It's obvious it was not God's will or you wouldn't be engaged to River."

Kareena didn't mean to go down this path, but she needed to get some things off her mind. She cared for River, even loved him, but her heart had always been with Stiles. One thing he said was true—it wasn't meant to be and she had to accept that.

"I love River. He's a good man, but—

"But what?"

"I am...or used to be...in love with you, Stiles. I don't know how I mistook your feelings for me. I just thought, well, I guess I wanted to believe you were in love with me too."

"Things happen, Kareena. Life doesn't always deal us the hand we want. But whatever it deals us we have to play that hand and play it to win. You're a great woman and I know you're going to make a wonderful wife to River."

"You're right, and the past is the past. There is no us and I've come to accept that. River and I will be walking down the aisle the end of the year, if God says the same."

"I believe He will. And for what it's worth, I'm sorry for any hurt I've caused you. I'm sorry for leading you on and giving you false hope that there could be anything more than friendship between us. Will you, can you, forgive me?"

Kareena looked at Stiles as tears formed and settled in the corners of her eyes. She nodded. "I have no choice. God commands us to forgive."

"This Beyond Burger is delish," Stiles said, taking a big bite of his burger then picking up some fries and popping them into his mouth. He couldn't remain on the subject of him and Kareena and what might have been or could have been. It was still a sensitive topic. He saw that when he saw the tears in her eyes and the tremble in her voice. Why was he the way he was?

"My sandwich is good too. Carl's Jr.'s food is always fresh and good though so I'm not surprised. Like Stiles, she knew it wasn't good for them to dwell on the past. She had a good man in her life. From this moment forward she was going to focus on giving all her love to him. River deserved that much. God had connected their paths and she was not going to let Stiles' issues rub off on her. She would always care about him, but hearing him, sitting across the desk from him, seeing his expression, was all she needed to know that it would take an act of God to tear down the walls he'd built around his heart.

"Did you hear anything about your high school friend who was murdered? Has anyone been arrested?"

Stiles shook his head. "Unfortunately, not, and to be honest I don't know how hard the MPD is looking. To them it's just another black man. I know it's not always the case, but most of the time it is, especially in Memphis."

"Did you see his wife?"

"Yes, I got a chance to visit her and the kids while I was there. She's still grieving. Leo was her everything. He was a good father, too. She misses him a lot and so do the kids. It's so sad. A man taken away from his family like that. I know he had his secrets and all, but he didn't deserve to die like that."

"It's so sad. The more I think about things, I believe you were right to take the position at Holy Rock. You're needed there. You can be there for Leo's widow and his kids. You can be there for your father and his wife, for your nephews, and your brother. I know your brother is still in a not-so-good space, but I believe in time things will change and get better."

"He's facing fed time, too. That has to weigh heavy on him. I know it would if it were me. The man is no saint, but he's a child of God and I still believe he loves the Lord. Things have to work out for my family. They just have to. And Fancy, his ex-wife, is dealing with it from all directions. That woman is a strong sista, I'm telling you."

"Even more reason it makes sense that you need to be there."

"Thanks, Kareena." He took another bite of his food and for the next fifteen minutes, they ate, laughed, and talked, staying away from any more sensitive conversations.

All in all, it was good to be back home.

14

"Trust takes years to build, seconds to break, and forever to repair." Comforting Quotes

*F*ancy stepped out into the warm welcoming sunshine with a new boldness. No more crying. No more being depressed about life. No more giving in to the negativity that tried to attack her mind over and over. She was a on a new mission in life.

"I'm on my way," she told Victoria.

She climbed inside her Benz GLC, put the luxury ride in reverse until she was on the street. Putting the pedal to the metal, a smile came over her as she said aloud, "I'm facing my truth because it's my time and no matter what's put in my way, it's going to be okay."

"I'm so glad you're finally out of that funk. I don't like it when you're down in your spirit," Victoria said. Fancy and Victoria had become basically best friends. Tara was still both of their friends but Tara had a husband and kids. She didn't have the freedom nor did she want to live the kind of life Victoria and Fancy led. Victoria and Fancy were two single women with adult children, no babies underfoot. Victoria helped Fancy realize that she had a lot to offer the world. She was a sassy, smart, sophisticated woman who deserved the best in life, and she was determined to live her best life now.

"To the mall first?"

"Yes, let's do this," Victoria said when she got inside Fancy's car. "It's the weekend baby, and I've got my best friend back! Yayyyy!"

"Girl, you are so silly."

Fancy and Victoria hung out all day and well into the evening. After shopping and buying several new outfits, they went to the spa and got the royal treatment. After leaving the spa, they dined at a fine dining restaurant. They caught the attention of several men at the mall and at the restaurant. While they were eating, Fancy saw some of the men who were with their wives or significant others, sneaking a look at her. She welcomed the attention. When they were at the mall, they even shared their phone numbers with a couple of eligible bachelors they met. They laughed and giggled like they were teenagers again. All in all, Fancy felt amazing. No more looking back. It was time to see what she'd been missing in life.

When she arrived home later that evening, she was exhausted but she didn't regret a single moment of the day. She took off her clothes down to her undies then went into the kitchen and poured herself a glass of white wine.

She took the wine and went into the family room. Her tablet was sitting on the table. She picked it up, powered it on, and prepared to start back on the book she had been reading. After reading a few chapters, she turned on the television. The ten o'clock news was coming on. She rarely watched the news. There was too much negativity and bad news. She often prayed that Memphis would have a revival and the violence and crime would stop. She surfed for a few minutes and then came across another local news station. She paused when she saw the picture of Deacon Leo. Turning the television volume up, placing the remote next to her and putting the tablet on the table, she listened to the reporter.

"I'm standing outside the bar where Leo Jones, a husband and father of two was beaten to death this past May. Crimestoppers, along with donations from Holy Rock Ministries, the church where Jones was a longtime deacon, is offering a $15,000 reward for information leading to the arrest and conviction of the person or persons who committed this heinous crime. Jones was well-liked and respected in the community. He worked with the youth at his church. We learned just before going on the air, a suspect has been detained in the case. We do not know if it was a crime stopper's tip responsible for this suspect's arrest at this time. We'll keep you updated as we learn more about this individual and what led to his arrest. Reporting, Bernard Abbott, News Channel 18."

Fancy looked next to where she was sitting for her phone but it wasn't there. "Phooey, left it in my purse." She stood up and went to her closet, found her purse, looked inside, and removed her phone.

She dialed the number and listened to it ring. After several rings it rolled over to voicemail. "Stiles, it's Fancy. Give me a call when you can. I just saw on the news they've arrested someone for Leo Jones' murder."

Sunday morning Pepper arrived at church for the second service. She arrived early so she could be sure to secure a good seat. She hated it when folks thought just because they sat in a certain seat on a regular basis that it somehow belonged to them. Wrong. She walked in, looked toward the front of the sanctuary for Xavier, but she didn't see him. She remained standing inside one of the three doorways at the rear of the church as people passed by pouring into Holy Rock. She finally saw him coming in through the side doors heading for his usual seat. She walked up the aisle and soon as he took his seat, she planted herself next to him before anyone had a chance to sit next to him.

He stared, complete surprise on his face. They hadn't talked much and they hadn't seen each other since their disagreement. She had hoped in her absence he would miss her enough where he would call and ask to see her, but that hadn't been the case. It was probably because Ian had snagged his nails into her man. She had to do something about that before all she'd done to bring Xavier to her side was for naught.

"Hey there." She leaned in and gave him a light kiss on the cheek.

"Hey. I'm surprised to see you." His brows flickered a little.

"Why? It's not like I don't come to church at all. I'm just not here every time the doors swing open like some people I know." She laughed while Xavier continued to stare.

"Why are you looking at me like that? Aren't you glad to see me?"

"Uh, sure."

Pepper looked up when she saw Ian appear. With a slick smile on her face, she spoke. "Hi, Ian."

"Uhh, hi, Pepper. What are you doing here? I thought demons were allergic to church."

"Then the question should be what are *you* doing here?" she shot back.

He rolled his eyes and then took a seat on the other side of Xavier.

"This is not the time or place you two."

"I agree. I'm here to enjoy today's services. I need a word from the Lord. I'm not going to allow the devil to get me upset," Pepper said, reaching over and squeezing Xavier's hand.

Ian tried to hold back his dislike of Pepper but she made it difficult, sometimes downright impossible. But they were in church and he understood that he had to keep it together.

"Hey, did you hear about them arresting a suspect in that man's beating death?"

Xavier looked at her. "What man?"

"You know, what's his name. The one who was a deacon here. I think he was a volunteer in the youth ministry, too."

"Deacon Jones? Leo Jones?"

"Yes, that's him."

"No, I hadn't heard. When did you hear that?"

"It popped up on my newsfeed this morning. I only stopped to read it when I saw the name Holy Rock on the feed."

Xavier removed his hand from underneath Pepper's and reached inside his pocket to retrieve his phone. The same as Pepper, when he opened his browser, the story popped up. Xavier read the article. There was a recent update showing the picture of a white male. It gave his name and age. He had a criminal background and was known to frequent gay bars looking for hookups. The article didn't come out and say it, but Xavier figured Leo had been one of those guys who took the bait and ended up dead. He didn't feel one way or the other about Leo's death. He was glad the man was dead and wouldn't be in his life anymore. But there were other things no one knew about that caused him to become uneasy.

"Interesting," Ian said as he looked at Xavier's phone. "I wonder what led to his arrest?"

"I don't know."

"I'm sure we'll hear more about it since they've found the one responsible," Pepper said, as if reassuring Xavier the killer would get his due justice.

What made Xavier nervous was learning they had arrested a suspect. He gave Ian a look that said what their mouths couldn't.

After church was over, Pepper invited Xavier to lunch, but he refused. "I'm staying for the next service."

"Yea, and after that we have plans." Ian couldn't wait to speak up and burst her little bubble.

Maintaining her composure, Pepper grabbed hold of Xavier's hand again, and again kissed him on the cheek. "You two have fun. We'll talk later," she said confidently as she swished off.

15

*"For it is disgraceful even to speak of the things
which are done by them in secret."*
Ephesians 5:12 NASB

*X*avier left Holy Rock after the last service and met Ian at Ian's apartment. The two young men searched online to see what else was being said, if anything, about Leo's brutal murder.

"It's probably only a matter of time before we get a visit from homicide detectives."

"I doubt it. You know they already talked to several members at Holy Rock, including his wife and me too since I'm the youth director. They talked to Khalil, too. After that as far as I know, no one else that I know has heard anything else from them. So why would they have more questions?"

"Because, you and I both know you and Leo had words that night."

"Yea, but I didn't kill him. Neither did you."

"But we went to the club that night."

"No, not really. We were *outside* of the club. I never went inside."

"Right, because you got cold feet."

"No, because I saw Leo coming out of the club. How do you think it made me feel to see that low life bastard? It proved he was who I knew he was."

"Yea, on the down low. Dudes like that kill me. Living two lives. His poor wife thinking he's God's answer to prayer but yet he's going behind her back having gay affairs, not man enough to admit what he is."

It was early afternoon, but it didn't stop Ian for making Xavier a shot of tequila. If he could get him to drink it, it would help him relax, and the added benefit would be Ian hoped to get Xavier back in his bed. Something he hadn't been able to do since there trip to New Orleans.

Xavier put his head in his hands as he sat down at Ian's table and started sobbing. "To have him call me all those gay slurs, and to talk about me and you like we were the scum of the earth. I was so mad. At that moment I wished he was dead. I couldn't help it. I was sick of his big mouth. That's why I punched him."

"Here. Drink this."

"I don't want it." Xavier shook his head.

"Come on, it'll help you relax."

"I can't believe what I did."

"Okay, so you laid one on him, that you did, Xavier. He deserved it. But you didn't kill him. We left him there. He had a bloody nose but he was alive and still cursing us out. I don't know if that guy they arrested will remember that or not, but he's the one they arrested, not us. And that's because we didn't do anything. You didn't do anything."

Xavier turned up the shot of tequila. "Do you think they had surveillance cameras?"

"Man, will you chill?" Ian poured another shot into the glass. "You're freaking out about nothing. Remember, when it first happened the news said there were surveillance cameras across the street but they weren't working. Even if they were, it wouldn't prove you or I had anything to do with that pervert being dead."

Xavier needed no prompting this time. He turned up the shot of tequila, then a third one. "But that guy they arrested saw us. He came out behind Leo. He helped him get up off the ground."

"And?"

"So what if he tells the cops about us?"

"He doesn't know us, Xavier. He probably couldn't even describe us anyway. Plus, we had already gotten in the car when he came out."

"I looked him dead in the eye. The dude laughed when Leo told me I was a walking dead man. I'm scared, Ian. I'm scared he might be able to describe me, maybe not you."

"Look, Xavier, I've been to that club a thousand times, and I've never seen that dude—ever. But even if he saw me, he doesn't know who I am. And you, well you never went inside. There was no one else on the streets around the club that night. At least not when you and Leo got into it. So, come on, get it together, man. You're freaking out for nothing."

Xavier started sobbing like a baby. "I don't want to go to prison, Ian. I can't go to prison."

Ian got up from where he was seated and walked over to Xavier, and stood behind him while Xavier remained seated. Ian wrapped his arms around him.

"Come on, Xavier. I'm telling you. You're not going to prison. You didn't do anything. Whatever happened after we left we don't know.

But it seems like Leo messed with the wrong guy. Whatever it was that made dude or whoever beat him to death, you better believe he deserved it. I don't feel sorry for what happened to him. If I feel sorry for anybody it would be his poor unsuspecting wife and his kids. That's it."

"I should have left this god forsaken city. I hate this place. Nothing good has come to me by staying here. First, I ruined Raymone's life. Thanks to me he'll never walk again, never be able to live on his own, nothing. My father hates me because I'm gay. My mother doesn't want to own up to the fact that I'm gay, and neither does my brother. I'm sick of it all. I'm sick of everything and everybody." Xavier continued to sob. He got up, pushing the chair back, almost knocking Ian to the floor. "I've got to go."

"Wait, where are you going? You don't need to leave like this, Xavier. You're too upset."

Xavier didn't seem to hear anything Ian was saying. He continued walking at a quickened pace toward the front door. He opened it and ran out, not stopping until he made it to his car

"Xavier, wait!" Ian yelled. "Come back, Xavier!"

Xavier unlocked the door with his key FOB, got inside his car, and sped away, leaving Ian standing in the doorway. He watched as Xavier drove out of the apartment parking lot and on to the street before closing his door.

Xavier accelerated. A car horn blared but he didn't seem to notice. His cell phone started ringing. It was Pepper, but he didn't answer. Ian called and again Xavier didn't answer the calls.

Pepper sent him a text. "Call me will you? We need to talk."

Ian followed up with his own text messages. "Xavier, come back. Everything will be okay. Please call me."

Xavier drove up Winchester Road at speeds that began to escalate. 60...70...80...90 miles. As he approached a nearby construction area in the street, he didn't slow his roll. He kept driving, blinded by wild thoughts playing in his mind about how worthless his life was and how much he'd screwed up. Horns blared incessantly. He didn't stop nor did he slow down as the car ran over a deep pot hole in the street. There was a booming sound, like an explosion. The silver Dodge Challenger went out of control, rammed into the concrete embankment, sending it catapulting into the air.

Pepper's patience was at its end. She'd texted and called repeatedly but there was no response from Xavier. She grabbed her keys and rushed out of the door. She couldn't put things off any longer. It was time she confronted Xavier face to face. It was the only way she could get him to understand the two of them were meant to be together.

Xavier could provide her with a good life. With the money his family had from the success and growth of Holy Rock, she witnessed firsthand the ease of living that could be enjoyed by her if she became Mrs. Xavier McCoy. She would be the perfect trophy wife. Yes, his family had issues, some unpleasant things that happened, but the benefits for her if she and Xavier married would far outweigh the family dysfunction.

On her drive to Xavier's apartment she envisioned the two of them happily married, living in a big house, with nice cars, no money worries, and of course she would have to get pregnant right away. That would seal the deal for her marriage. He was not the type of guy who would abandon his wife and kids. He was a good guy, just confused about his sexuality, but that was an easy fix in Pepper's mind. His attraction to her was evident by the way he treated her and the way he made love to her when they were together. Ian was not going to win. No way. Not now. Not ever.

16

*"Deep inside us, we know what every family
therapist knows: the problems between the
parents become the problems within the
children." Roger Gould*

Khalil couldn't get his father's pop-up visit
out of his mind. The man was a piece of work.
Not only did he barge into Holy Rock ready to
expose his own son, and belittle his mother,
once again Hezekiah had shown he had no
regard for the well-being of his family. Did he
ever love them, because the loyalty he showed
toward them was nonexistent. It showed in
everything he did to them, starting with how he
practically threw his mother out of their home
and slept with Detria behind her back. He was
scum. All he seemed to care about was the 100
grand Khalil had taken from him. Money was
always his issue. It's what had gotten him and
Fancy prison time when Khalil and Xavier were
kids. It's what was going to put him back behind
bars once he went to trial and was found guilty.
That would be the best day of Khalil's life, and
Khalil couldn't wait to see it happen.

As for the present, after Hezekiah's threats,
Khalil knew more than ever he had to watch his
back. After the scene Hezekiah made at Holy
Rock, he didn't put anything past the man. He'd
already had those guys to ransack his
apartment and vandalize his car. God only

knows what could have happened to him had he not been able to get away from them that night.

He called Omar. "Hey, can you meet me at my place later this evening?"

"Sure, but I probably won't be leaving from here until seven or eight."

"Is everything all right?"

"Oh, yeah. Just have to make sure the guys get all the light bulbs and filters changed. Holy Rock is no small church and the ceilings are so high that it takes a lot of time and, well you know what I'm saying. Anyway, once I go over everything that I expect to be done with the crew, I'll head your way."

"Is Reggie there?"

"Yea, I'm going to leave him in charge. He'll make sure everything is done as it should be."

"Cool."

"Hey, you all right?"

"I will be. See you later, bruh."

"Ok. I'm out." Omar ended the call and returned to his duties. He knew Khalil well. Something in his voice told Omar that something was going on with his friend. Khalil sounded worried and uptight. That could only mean his ol' man had started stirring up more trouble. It had already floated around Holy Rock about Hezekiah McCoy's visit and their being a big blowout. Omar and Khalil hadn't had a chance to sit down and talk about it. They'd only exchanged a few text messages but nothing in detail, but it was enough for Omar to piece together that Hezekiah had stirred up trouble.

There was a time Omar looked up to and respected Pastor Hezekiah McCoy as being a genuine man of God, but every day he seemed to learn more and more how vicious and gangster the guy who once stood behind the pulpit of Holy Rock was. The man camped behind enemy lines.

Omar's loyalty was with Khalil. He was down with helping him in any way he could. After all, Khalil had been there for him during some of Omar's hard times. He'd helped him out financially when Omar lost his job and had problems making rent and providing for his family. When he stepped into the role of senior pastor of Holy Rock, Khalil immediately called Omar and hired him to be Holy Rock's maintenance supervisor. He paid him darn good money. Not only was Khalil there for him financially, enabling him to provide well for his wife and kids, Khalil was always there for moral support. Their friendship was real and their bond was tight.

"What do you want to do about it?" Omar asked as he and Khalil sat in Khalil's man cave slash media room drinking beer while a basketball game played on the 75-inch UHD TV.

"I know I have to watch my back. I don't know when his trial is coming up. Probably sometime this year, but I can't wait on the Feds to put him behind bars. I have to do something now."

"Yeah, but what? You have any ideas?"

"I need to hit him where it hurts—his pockets."

"I hear ya, but let me say this. I think you need to hire some bodyguards, security. You know what I mean?"

Khalil nodded.

"Just like you have armor bearers who look out for you at Holy Rock, you need dudes who bear arms outside of Holy Rock. You know, some real life bodyguards and not just for you, but for your mom too, even your brother. If your ol' man is out for your blood, I don't see him stopping short of laying you down, bruh. I hate to think a father would do that to his own son, but it's real. It happens, you know. Shhh...look what happened already with those dudes who tried to do something bad to you. You said he was responsible for that, and now dude comes to Holy Rock live and in person making threats toward you and your family.

"Right...right." Khalil nodded in agreement. "Let's work on it then. First thing tomorrow, we'll get some guys in place. But I'm telling you, I'm not done with him. I've got to find a way to exact my own justice on him, and I got to do it soon."

"Whoa, look at that fool." Omar jumped out of the movie style recliner. "LeBron fouled dude and the ref didn't call it?"

"That's my boy." Khalil leaned back in his recliner and laughed. "LeBron is the GOAT. For real."

"Nah, I don't think so," Omar countered.

For the remainder of the evening Khalil tried to take his mind off his father and the two friends enjoyed the game.

17

"Anger and hate against ones we love steals our hearts but contempt or pity leaves us silent and ashamed." Izquotes

"Good morning, Eliana. Good morning, ladies." Khalil smiled as he walked into Holy Rock the following morning.

"Good morning, Pastor Khalil," Eliana and the other ladies answered.

"Eliana, I need to see you in my office."

Sista Mavis crooked her neck so she could hear the conversation between the two. She suspected there was something more than admin and pastor relationship between those two. Eliana hadn't denied her feelings for Pastor Khalil when Sista Mavis tried to steer her toward Stiles. It was easy to see from her expression, the tone of her voice, and the way she talked about Khalil that Eliana was head over heels for him.

Sista Mavis thought about it. Maybe Pastor Stiles was not the man for Eliana. Maybe he needed someone more his age. Who had the patience to deal with him and his sensitive emotions. Maybe it wouldn't be such a bad thing if the girl set her sights on Pastor K. Looking at Pastor K and Eliana, they kinda *would* make a cute couple. They were young, loved the Lord, and they possessed great personalities, but Pastor K had dropped a couple of notches on

Sista Mavis' poll after what happened when Pastor Hezekiah came to Holy Rock.

Sista Mavis watched Eliana move from behind her desk, pick up her tablet, and follow Pastor K up the hall to his office. The disturbance Pastor K caused the other day was still present in Sista Mavis' mind. She was disturbed by what she expected to be a pleasant meeting between son and father but had turned into an all-out fiasco. It was the one time she'd witnessed Pastor K's temper, and it turned her off a little because no child, young or old, for any reason, should disrespect their parents the way Pastor Khalil had done. She heard their voices, especially Khalil's screaming at his father, and it wasn't a good thing. Their voices could be heard all the way up to the front of the church office.

When Hezekiah appeared back in the front of the office, Sista Mavis could easily tell that he was angry. He didn't even tell her goodbye. And Khalil, that boy said some terrible things to his father. He looked so much like his mother. Sista Mavis wondered if Fancy McCoy had poisoned her sons' minds against their father.

Khalil pulled Eliana into his arms as soon as he closed the door to his office. He kissed her, not holding back his desire and need for her.

Eliana returned his kiss. Being in his arms was where she wanted to be. His kisses set her on fire and stirred up feelings she hadn't felt for anyone else before him. God, she wanted to be his wife so badly. She tried not to think that far ahead, but every night when she prayed, she asked God to give her a husband. She went one step farther and prayed that if it was God's will, that man would be Khalil McCoy.

Khalil scooped her into his arms and walked her backward over to his desk. He sat her on the edge of his desk, removed her tablet from her hands, and set it on the side of her. Their kisses grew with intensity as she allowed his hands to freely roam.

Wrapping her arms around his neck she gave him as much access to her body as possible.

"We can't," she said, as her breathing grew heavy and tiny moans escaped from between her lips. "Not here."

Khalil pulled back. Both of their faces flushed. "I know," he said, his breath just as heavy as hers. He helped her down and she stood before him.

"I can't get enough of you, Eliana."

Eliana turned red as she blushed.

Khalil planted his hands around her tiny waist and closed the space between them as he kissed her again.

"Okay, okay," he said, stepping back. "I have to restrain myself."

"Yes, you do." She smiled. "Now, let's go over your schedule for the day."

Khalil strained to walk behind his desk. He pulled out the office chair and took a seat while Eliana moved her chair closer to his desk and sat down too.

Grabbing her tablet off his desk, she powered it on. As much as he wanted to throw caution to the wind, get up, grab her, and make love to her, this was neither the time nor place. He had too much he had to do. He was making so much money, or rather Holy Rock Ministries was making so much money, Khalil was fast becoming a wealthy man. The social media ministry was a huge success and the viewership continued to grow by leaps and bounds. The television ministry was growing as well with it not only being live on Sunday and during midweek services, but it was repeated during the wee hours of the morning on two channels to reach those people who normally surfed during those hours. People from all over the U.S. were becoming partners in his ministry. It was working too. The money was flowing in nonstop and Khalil's pockets grew fatter and fatter. Had he desired to, he could easily have given his father back the 100 grand, and then some, without missing it.

Weekly and Sunday worship had tripled and sometimes upwards of fifty people or more walked down the aisles of Holy Rock at one service alone to give their lives to Christ, to seek prayer, or join the church by Christian experience. It was mind-boggling. He was not about to allow his father to destroy that.

"I need you to create a job description and a job post for men or women who are interested in joining the security team."

"You want to increase security? Any reason?" she asked. "I'm just saying, you have a good group of men and women already. More than enough, really."

"Yeah, that's here at Holy Rock. But after that little move my father made the other day, I think it would be wise to have security for me and my mother when we are outside of Holy Rock. Oh, and my brother, too. And it's not only because of my father. More people are beginning to recognize me. That means more crazies out there. I don't need some fool pulling up on me with stupid thoughts. Make sure it states this is for a private security team, not for Holy Rock. I want you to do some research about what the starting salary should be. I want them paid well. Only the best with impeccable backgrounds and references. And I don't want to see them or interview them until you've covered all bases."

"Gotcha," Eliana, said, nodding as she entered the information on her tablet. She fully agreed and understood where Khalil was coming from. Memphis had become a violent city and it was getting worse every day. Rarely did a day pass when there wasn't a murder, shooting, or some other form of violence taking place. Now that his face was plastered on television all times of day and night, he was right, the more recognizable he was. She couldn't have her future husband harmed in any way.

In the middle of his and Eliana's meeting, Khalil's cell phone rang. He answered and listened.

Eliana watched Khalil's face turn to a dark purplish color. His free hand went to his head as he stood from the chair and with speed moved from behind his desk.

"Thank you again. I'm on my way."

"Khalil, what's wrong? You've turned two shades darker."

"It's my brother. He was in a bad accident. He's at Regional One in the trauma center. Will you call my mother? Wait, on second thought. I'll call her after I get to the hospital and see how he is."

"I'm coming with you," Eliana said, without asking.

Surprising to her, Khalil didn't rebuff her. "Come on then," he said. "Let's go."

As they passed the front office, Eliana quickly told Sista Mavis she and Pastor Khalil would be gone for the day, that there'd been an emergency. "I'll call you from the car and explain.

Sista Mavis saw the fright on both of their faces as they hurried out of the church. She ran to the door and watched as Pastor Khalil followed Eliana to her assigned parking space. The two got into her car and sped off the church parking lot.

Something had happened and whatever it was, Sista Mavis had a feeling it wasn't good. Wasn't good at all.

18

"It's hard to watch your life unfold, and sad. Life changes." Cilla Black

*E*liana stopped and let Khalil out of the car at the entrance to the hospital's trauma center. "I'll be in as soon as I park."

Khalil threw up a hand as he closed the car door and then sprinted toward the entrance.

Inside the trauma center, he rushed up to the patient information desk and inquired about his brother.

"He's being worked on now. No visitors are allowed at this time," the receptionist informed him.

"Can you at least tell me how he is?"

"All I can tell you is they're still working on him. Please go to the Trauma Waiting Room. The doctor will call you from a phone inside the room as soon as he has something to report."

"Where's the waiting room?"

The woman pointed to her right. "It's up that hallway and to the right. You'll see the sign."

"Thanks." Khalil walked down the hallway but stopped when he heard his name called.

"Khalil," Eliana said, briskly walking toward him.

She caught up to him and together they walked up the hallway while he told her what the receptionist shared about Xavier.

"He's going to be okay. God is a healer and a restorer. You know that," Eliana assured him as she rubbed his back in a circular motion.

"There it is," he pointed to the sign that read *Trauma Unit Waiting Room*. He opened the door but stopped dead in his tracks when he saw Hezekiah.

"What are you doing here?" he asked, disregarding three other people sitting in the room who looked at him strangely.

"Why do you think I'm here? My baby boy is back there," Hezekiah answered with frustration laced in his voice.

Eliana tugged on Khalil's arm. "Don't make a scene," she whispered.

"You've got some nerve."

"Now is not the time nor place for any foolishness from you, son. I'm here because my son has been in a terrible accident. The same as I would be if it were you."

"I doubt you would be here for me. You and I both know that."

Khalil shook his head as Eliana walked a step ahead of him as a way of guiding him to a nearby row of empty seats. She sat down and then looked at Khalil. "Pastor, please, sit down."

Khalil followed her prompt and took the seat next to her while maintaining a transfixed stare at his father.

There was a young lady sitting next to Hezekiah who looked somewhat frightened as she tightened her hold on a small child sitting on her lap. Eliana didn't know if the woman was with Hezekiah or just happened to be sitting next to him because of where Hezekiah had parked his wheelchair. She did, however, recognize the man seated on the other side of the woman. It was the same man who picked up Hezekiah from Holy Rock the other day.

"Hello, Miss," Hezekiah said, acknowledging Eliana.

"Hello, Pastor McCoy," Eliana replied and then focused her eyes on the television screen mounted on the wall in front of her.

"Where's your mother?"

"She's not here."

"I can see she's not here? Why?"

"Not that it's any of your business, she doesn't know."

"What?"

"You heard me. She doesn't know. I haven't told her."

"What do you mean you haven't told her? For God's sake, her baby boy is laid up in the trauma center in critical condition and you haven't told your mother?"

"Wait a minute. How do you know he's in critical condition? Have you seen the doctor? A nurse?"

"I *am* his father, so of course I've talked to the doctor. You may not like that, but it is what it is and I am who I am."

Eliana wondered how Hezekiah found out about the accident before Khalil.

Just then the phone in the waiting room started ringing. "Answer that, Isabella," Hezekiah said to the woman.

The man who Eliana recognized picked up the phone and passed it to the woman.

"Hello." Her voice was timid, almost childlike. "Yes, just a minute."

"They're asking for you," she said.

Hezekiah pushed the button on his power chair and rolled over to the woman. She pushed the phone toward him and Hezekiah received it.

"Hello. Yes, this is Hezekiah McCoy. How is he?"

Khalil watched, finding it difficult to remain poised. Here this man was who appeared out of the woodwork and the doctor was talking to him about his little's brother condition. Khalil didn't like. He didn't like it one bit.

Again, Eliana sensing his tension, reached over and gave his hand a tight squeeze.

Isabella stole a glance at the couple. Khalil had features just like Hezekiah. She already surmised that he had his daddy's ways by the way he barged in exerting his authority. She could see the girl with him had some strong feelings for him. It was written all over her face. Maybe one day she would have someone who made her want to willingly be by his side, love him, and care for him. Her child squirmed until he broke loose from his mother and ran toward a stranger sitting on the opposite side of the room.

"Come back here. Don't go over there," Isabella admonished. Before she could fully stand and step past Hezekiah, the kid darted toward Eliana and plopped his head in her lap.

Eliana laughed, patted the cute little boy on his head, and then began talking to him.

Isabella rushed over. "I'm sorry."

"Oh, no need to apologize. I love kids, and he is adorable."

"Thank you." Isabella picked up the boy who immediately struggled against his mother. "Stop it before you get a spanking."

The boy stopped squirming and allowed his mother to put him down on the floor. She reached for his hand and led him back to their seat while he looked back at Eliana.

Children was another reason Eliana was ready to get married. She wanted at least three, maybe even four. She had the idyllic dream planted in her head of how perfect life would be with her being a wife and mother, living in a big house with a man who loved, worshipped, and adored her. Maybe she was crazy to believe that dream could come true with Khalil, but nonetheless, she felt it was her truth and this was her turn and her time to do everything she could to make that dream into a reality.

"What did he say?" she heard Khalil ask his father, bringing her out of her daydream.

"They're going to let me get a quick glimpse of him as soon as they get him cleaned up. He's on a ventilator. Lungs collapsed, fractured bones in his face and he fractured his pelvis. They think he might have internal bleeding. They're going to take him to surgery and run more tests."

Khalil looked over at Eliana. "I've got to call my mother."

Hezekiah heard what he told the attractive young woman. He figured she was more than just his son's administrative assistant, she was probably his boo. She looked like his type. The way she kept holding on to his hand and looking into his eyes, yeah, Hezekiah knew Khalil was tapping that.

"I think that's a good idea. Fancy's going to be furious when she finds out you didn't tell her Xavier is laid up in a hospital," Hezekiah said to his son.

"This is family business. What I do or do not do doesn't concern you anymore."

The phone rang again and they stopped talking. Benny picked the phone up once again. This time he motioned for one of the other people in the room waiting on news of the condition of their family member or loved one. "Are you the family of Carson?"

The brunette, blue eyed woman nodded.

"It's for you," he said to her.

She got up, walked to the phone and Benny pushed it gently into her hand.

The woman listened to whatever was being said. "Thank you," she said and hung up the phone. She went back over to where she was seated, picked up her purse, and exited the waiting room.

"Suit yourself, but you should know your mother and how she's going to react."

"Do you want me to call?" Eliana asked.

"No, I'll do it. I'm going to step out into the hall. I'll be right back."

"Okay," replied Eliana.

Xavier stood up and exited the waiting room. Once outside the room he called Omar, explained what had gone down, and asked him to go pick up his mother and bring her to the hospital.

Without hesitation, Omar's reply was, "I gotcha. Tell her I'm on my way. I'll call her when I get to the gate."

"Thanks, O."

Next, Khalil called his mother.

Fancy was enjoying a quiet, non-eventful evening at home, reading and watching a little reality TV, when her cell phone rang, jarring her from her relaxed state of mind.

She looked at the phone screen. "Khalil, hi, honey. What's going on with you?"

"Ma, I'm at Regional One."

"Regional One? As in hospital?"

"Yes."

"What are you doing there? You usually leave sick visits to the ministerial staff. Someone must have specifically requested to see you."

"No, it's nothing like that."

"Then what is it?" *Pause.* "Honey, are you okay? You're making me nervous." She began patting her hand on her knee.

"Yes, I'm fine, Ma."

"Then what's going on? What are you doing at Regional One?"

"Ma, it's—"

"It's who? What's going on, Khalil?" She placed her hand on her belly as it suddenly knotted up. She stood up from the sofa.

"Ma, Omar's on his way to pick you up. Xavier was in an accident."

"Oh, my God! Is he all right?" She nervously ran into her room and started taking off the clothes she had on. She rummaged through her closet to find something to put on.

"Well, they haven't let me see him yet. He's in the trauma center. They're still working on him though." He didn't want to tell her the extent of his brother's injuries over the phone. She already sounded like she was about to fall apart. His father was right about one thing; he should have told his mother about Xavier's accident from the very beginning.

"I'm getting dressed. I'll be there as soon as I can."

"Ma, I told you, Omar is on his way. He should be there in a few minutes."

"When did this happen?"

"Ma, we'll talk when you get here. Just get ready. Tell Omar to let you out at the entrance to the Trauma Center. We're in the Trauma Center Waiting Room."

Fancy was shaking life a leaf. "Okay, I'm getting dressed while I'm talking to you. But did you say 'we'? Who's there with you?"

Khalil spoke before thinking. "Eliana....and....and Dad."

"What did you say?" Fancy was stepping into a pair of charcoal brown cuffed ankle slacks but stopped midstream when she heard Khalil say Hezekiah was there.

"He was here when we got here. I don't know how he found out about it, but he did, and he's in the waiting room."

"I don't want him anywhere near my son, Khalil." Fancy's blood boiled. "What in the heck was Hezekiah doing at the hospital? Hadn't he caused enough trouble?"

"Ma, don't worry about Dad. Just get ready and wait for Omar."

Eliana stepped out into the hall. "The doctor called back. You can see Xavier but only for a few minutes."

Hezekiah rolled up to the door and Benny ran up beside him and opened it. He almost ran into Eliana as she partially blocked the door.

"I'm sorry, sweetheart," he apologized as Eliana quickly stepped to the side and out of Hezekiah's way.

"Ma, I gotta go. They're going to let us see Xavier for a few minutes. I'll see you when you get here."

"Please, tell my baby, I'm on the way."

"I will, Ma." Khalil ended the call.

Fancy couldn't contain herself. What had happened to Xavier? What kind of accident had he been involved in? "Oh, God, please let him be okay. Please, God." She finished dressing and continued to pray aloud while pacing the floor, waiting on Omar.

Omar arrived shortly after she finished talking to Khalil. "First Lady, I'm here," he said when she answered the call from the entrance of Lion's Gate.

She buzzed him in and the gate slowly opened.

Omar sped through the private, quiet and secluded neighborhood until he arrived at Fancy's house. He was about to get out of the car to go knock on the door when the front door flew open and Fancy appeared. He stepped outside of his car.

"I'm coming. No need to come up here." Fancy turned, locked her door, ran down the steps and dashed to Omar's car. He darted to the passenger's side and opened the door for her.

"Thank you. Now please, get me to the hospital. I have to get to my son."

19

"Love can change a person the way a parent can change a baby - awkwardly, and often with a great deal of mess." Lemony Snicket

*H*ezekiah was allowed into Xavier's room first. Khalil wished he had the power to stop him from seeing Xavier, but there was nothing he could do about it. Hezekiah *was* Xavier's father so he was given priority over Khalil.

Xavier lay in the hospital bed, his face bruised and swollen so big it looked like a basketball. His eyes were swollen shut.

Hezekiah couldn't tell if his son was conscious or not.

"Xavier, son, it's your father." He rolled up closer to his son's bedside, and took hold of his swollen hand. "Everything is going to be all right. You're going to make it through this. God's gotcha."

Xavier, under heavy sedation, imagined he heard his father's voice. He was in a dreamlike state of mind, not able to differentiate what was real or a ploy his mind was playing on him. He couldn't move, couldn't open his eyes, but he was not in pain. He heard the voice again. Where was he? Was he dead? What had happened to him? Was he dreaming?

"I'm praying for you, son. I know I've said and done some things that were wrong, but I'm still your father. And though I haven't said it much, if at all, I love you."

He looked on at Xavier, saw the tubes inside his mouth and nose, watched the ventilator as it took every breath for his son. He looked at the monitors, the IV, everything and then back at Xavier. Xavier looked like he'd been in the world's worst boxing match.

For the first time since he couldn't recall, tears crested in the corner of Hezekiah's eyes. "God, bring him through this," he prayed as he held on to his son's hand. "Forgive me for being less than the father you would have me to be, dear Lord. But don't punish my son for my mistakes, God. Heal him. Bring him through—"

A nurse walked in while he was praying. "I'm sorry, but they're on the way to get him to take him to surgery."

Hezekiah looked at the nurse and nodded. "I love you, son."

Khalil appeared in the room.

"Sir, you can only stay a couple of minutes. We're about to take him to surgery."

"Yes, ma'am. I understand. Thank you." Khalil walked over to his brother, fighting back tears when he saw how bad he looked.

Hezekiah turned his chair around and rolled out of the room, giving the brothers some private time.

"Xavier, man, what did you get yourself into?"

Again, Xavier heard someone talking. This time it sounded like his brother but the words were nothing more than garbled sounds. Wherever he was, whatever state of mind he was in, he was euphoric, at peace. He saw a beaming, bright blue aura. It was like nothing he'd ever seen before. Whatever it was gave him a sense of overwhelming tranquility. He was worried about nothing and thought of no one, only concentrating on the blue aura shining brightly before him.

"Ma is on the way, bruh. We love you, and you know I'm praying for ya."

"Excuse me, sir. They're here to get him," the nurse walked into the room and told him.

Right behind her two attendants entered the room. "Excuse me," one of them told Khalil.

"Uh, sure." Khalil stepped aside. "Xavier, we're here. You're not alone," Khalil said before he walked out of the hospital room and into the hallway.

He and Hezekiah remained in the hallway, waiting until they saw Xavier being rolled away to surgery. Neither of them spoke a word to each other. Several more people stood, and some leaned against the wall in the hallway also waiting to see their loved ones. It looked like they were standing in a SNAP line.

A few minutes after stepping into the hallway, Khalil and Hezekiah watched as Xavier was wheeled out of the trauma bay and down the hospital corridor with one attendant steering the IV stand and the other attendant steering the hospital bed.

"Jehovah Rapha, be with him," Hezekiah said lowly as his son was wheeled past him.

Khalil followed behind them until they reached an elevator where he was told it was as far as he could go.

"You can wait in the waiting room. Someone will call and let you know how he's doing," one of the attendants said.

Khalil, head hung low, turned and walked back toward the waiting room. Hezekiah had disappeared. When he opened the door and entered the waiting room, he saw Hezekiah had returned to the room.

Eliana jumped up and ran over to Khalil. "How is he?" she asked although she clearly heard Hezekiah tell his friends that his son was in bad shape and they had taken him to surgery. She said nothing when she heard this, but waited on Khalil to return.

Khalil repeated basically the same thing she already heard, but he didn't say his brother was in bad shape. He didn't have to. Eliana could read it all over his face. Khalil was worried.

She squeezed his hand...again. "Do you want to go to the cafeteria and grab something to eat? I'm sure he's going to be in surgery for quite some time."

Khalil shook his head. "No, I'm good. I need to stay and look out for, Ma. She should be here soon. But you can go. You probably should get ready to go home. I can get Omar to take me to Holy Rock to pick up my ride or I'll call LYFT."

"No, I wouldn't think of leaving you. Not now. I want to be here for you," she whispered, hoping Hezekiah couldn't over hear her. It wasn't that she cared what he might think, but their relationship was private, for now. She wanted to respect that. If she had her way she would shout from the rooftops that she loved Khalil McCoy, but all things come in time.

"You must be hungry. And you probably should call Sista Mavis and let her know what's going on. We need the prayers of the saints. As much as that woman gossips, she's still a prayer warrior and she can get the word out so the church will be in prayer."

"Okay, I'll be back as soon as I can."

"This is a huge hospital. It may take you some time to find the cafeteria. I'll call you if something comes up."

"Sure." She had to stop herself when she almost leaned in and kissed him on the cheek.

Hezekiah noticed the quick move and smiled. *Yep, he's definitely hitting that.*

Eliana walked back toward the front of the trauma center to see if she could get directions to the hospital cafeteria. She saw Fancy rushing through the automatic doors. Their eyes locked.

"Eliana."

"Mrs. McCoy."

"Where's my son?"

"Come on, I'll show you where Khalil is. Xavier is in surgery. Khalil can tell you more."

As they hurried up the hallway toward the waiting room, Fancy began with her questions. "How long have you been here?"

"I drove Khalil here when we heard about the accident."

"What happened? What happened to my baby?"

"As far as I know, he was in a car accident. I haven't heard much else."

"When did it happen?"

Eliana wanted to be careful not to talk too much. She didn't want Fancy getting upset with

Khalil for not calling her. Had she been in Fancy's shoes and her child was lying in a hospital bed and no one had told her, she would be highly pissed, to say the least.

"I don't know what time it happened. But we've been here for a couple of hours. They wouldn't tell Khalil anything at first."

"Why didn't he call me? Why didn't *you* call me?"

"I, well, he didn't know how serious it was and I, well, I..."

Fancy threw up a hand, quickly dismissing anything else Eliana was about to say. "I don't care if he had a scrape on his pinky, I should have been told. Anyway, I'm here now. I'll handle Khalil later."

"Yes, ma'am."

"Were you about to leave? I saw you at the exit when I came in."

"No, I was about to ask someone where the hospital cafeteria is and then I saw you. Would you like me to bring you something back?"

"No, I'm good. Thank you. And, Eliana, for what it's worth, thank you for being here with my son. I shouldn't have bit your head off. You're only going to do what he says and that's fine, but he should have known better. He should have called me."

"I agree, and you're welcome. I wouldn't be any other place."

Fancy smiled. I'm sure you wouldn't."

They arrived at the waiting room. "Here it is. I'll be back as soon as I can."

"Okay. Thanks, sweetie." Fancy opened the door to the waiting room, walked inside, and closed it behind her.

Khalil stood up when he saw his mother enter the waiting room. There were a number of other people gathered in the waiting room. Three of them were sitting on the same row of seats as Hezekiah, a few others scattered at the far end of the room.

Khalil hugged his mother, but she barely reciprocated. Instead, her eyes zeroed in on Hezekiah. She pushed herself out of her son's arms and walked over to her ex-husband.

"Ma, don't," Khalil said, but of course she ignored him.

"What are you doing here?"

Isabella held on to her child as she stood up and moved to the other side of Benny and sat down.

"Honey, are you with him?" Fancy asked when she saw Isabella move.

Isabella nodded and responded, "Yes." Isabella had seen Fancy on several occasions when Isabella used to attend Holy Rock, but she'd never seen her up close and in her personal space. Fancy was beautiful, her make up flawless but natural looking, her hair laid, and she was impeccably dressed. She had an air of sophistication and self-assurance about her that Isabella immediately envied. She often dreamed of being a beautiful, powerful, assertive, and secure woman like she believed Fancy McCoy to be.

"Who are you? His li'l knock off?"

Isabella held her son tighter as he began to push against her arms and reach out to Fancy.

"No need to talk to her like that. You don't even know her. And for your information, she's my personal assistant and caregiver."

Fancy laughed aloud. "Humph, I just bet she is," she said still with her eyes glued on Isabella. "Is that his child?"

"Not that it's none of your business, but no, he's not," Hezekiah spoke up before Isabella had a chance to answer.

"Let me leave you alone. You don't know any better. You look like you're no older than my baby boy. But you," she turned toward Hezekiah, "you do know better. But I don't care what you do. I just want to know why you're here."

"I'm here for the same reason you're here. I don't want to argue with you, especially in front of a room full of people. If you want to show your behind you can do it all by yourself. My main focus is on our son and his well-being."

Fancy was quiet. It hit her. Hezekiah was right. This was neither the time nor the place to show how ignorant she could act. And truth be told, she was not the least bit interested in Hezekiah and his foolishness, or was she? She turned and walked away.

Khalil came up behind her and stood beside her. He put his arm around her shoulder and led her outside the waiting room.

"Come on, Ma." In the hall he tried to calm his mother. "Ma, settle down. I know you're upset about Dad being here, but it is what it is.

Leave it alone. You have enough worries. Don't let him add to it."

"I know. You're right. It's just that I can't believe he has the audacity to be here. He doesn't give a darn about Xavier or you. He's proven that over and over again."

"But it doesn't matter. What does matter is Xavier. If Dad wants to be here, then let him. Actually, after I got over the shock of seeing him here, I have to say that I'm glad he is here. At least it shows me he has a little bit of heart for his family left."

"I'm going to the nurses' station to see what they can tell me about my child. I can't wait on some darn phone to ring to tell me what they're doing to my baby."

"Ma, they said the doctor or nurse would call and keep us updated."

"Well, I want them to know that I'm here."

"Oh, okay. That's a good idea. So far, they've been keeping Dad informed. In their book, I don't matter since they know Hezekiah is Xavier's father. I mean, he's been telling me what they say when they call, but it's not the same as me hearing it for myself."

"Well, we'll see about that."

Fancy walked boldly up the hallway. Her heels clicking along the way, her gait heavy and steady. She didn't stop until she found the nurses' station and informed them of who she was. The nurse told her the same thing she'd told Khalil, they would be in touch with the family through the phone in the waiting room.

"I can tell you this much," the nurse said after checking something on the computer, "your son is still in surgery. And try not to worry. They will call you as often as necessary to keep you apprised of how he's doing."

Fancy didn't like it one bit, but she had no choice but to adhere to what the nurse told her. The woman was kind and seemed sympathetic toward Fancy, but protocol was protocol and she had to follow it

"Is there anything we can get you? Water, soda, coffee?" the nurse offered.

"No, but thank you," Fancy said and sighed before turning around and walking away.

"Thank you," Khalil told the nurse and then followed his mother back to the waiting room.

Fancy walked into the waiting room and took a seat.

Khalil's text notifier chimed. It was Omar. "Did First Lady find you?"

"Yeah, she's here. Was bout to text you and let u know."

"Need me to come up?"

"Nah. We good. Preciate you, man."

"No prob. I'ma head back to the crib. Sure you don't need me?"

"Nah, just need ur prayers. I'll let you know if anything comes up."

"Ok but if you need anything, I'm here for ya."

"Yea, I know."

Hezekiah sat across the room sneaking looks at Fancy and Khalil without them noticing. The longer he sat in the waiting room, the more he thought about his family. He was still hurt by their betrayal, but he began to realize that some things weren't worth the discord or the argument. One of those things was the money that was missing. He had no evidence Khalil was the one who'd taken it. For all he knew, it could have been George. Shucks, George had access to the condo the same as Khalil. He could have easily taken it before Khalil and Holy Rock reclaimed possession of the condo. Or it could have been that powder head, Detria. In his gut, however, he felt it was Khalil. Khalil had almost admitted it and he sure as heck hadn't denied it. He pushed the money thoughts aside. He had to focus his energy and thoughts on his own future. George would be getting released from the federal pen in 60 days, and Hezekiah could very well be exchanging places with him if he was found guilty of embezzlement.

The phone rang. Fancy jumped up. This time, Hezekiah was nearest the phone. "Hello. Hold on, please."

It was for one of the other people sitting in the waiting room.

Fancy sat back down and watched as a bald head, short and dumpy white man walked to the phone.

"Thank you," the man said to Hezekiah.

Eliana returned with a cup carrier holding three cups. "I know you said you didn't want anything, but I brought you something back anyway. They had sweet tea with lemon and Sprite zero."

"You're a sweetheart," Fancy said. She was beginning to have a real change of heart toward Eliana. She was just the kind of girl Khalil needed in his life. She was committed to him at work and now Fancy saw how she was even more dedicated to him outside of Holy Rock's walls. It was easy to sense that Eliana was in love with her son.

"Thanks, Eliana. Which one do you want, Ma?"

"I'll take the Sprite Zero." She looked at the top of the cup.

"Both of these are Sprite Zeroes," Eliana told her.

"Fancy removed one of the cups out of its holder.

Khalil removed the other cup filled with tea.

Eliana sat down and removed the last cup for herself. "I'll put the cup holder under my chair until we're done."

"Okay," Khalil said. "Thanks again, Eliana. This was right on time."

Eliana opened her MK tote and removed a bag containing sandwiches and chips. "They had a Subway down there so I bought back a turkey club sandwich and a veggie delite. Take your pick. I brought some candy bars back too." She reached back inside her purse and pulled out three candy bars and offered them to Khalil and Fancy.

"Ma?"

"I don't want anything, but that was thoughtful of you, Eliana. You seem to know exactly what my son likes."

Eliana blushed.

"Go ahead, eat both of them, Khalil. If I get hungry, I'll eat one of those candy bars, but right now my stomach is in knots. I'm just wondering what's taking so long for them to call and tell us about Xavier."

"They'll call soon, Ma. Try not to worry."

"That's easy for you to say. You wait until you become a parent." She glanced over at Eliana.

Eliana blushed again but remained silent as she looked away and returned the candy bars to her bag.

Khalil unwrapped the veggie sandwich first and began to gobble it. The smell and sight of it awakened his hunger.

Eliana opened the bag of plain potato chips and passed them to him.

Isabella got up, picked up her child, and walked past them and out the door, leaving Benny and Hezekiah.

The phone rang shortly after she left. This time when Hezekiah answered, Fancy watched and listened. She heard him say, "Yes, this is Hezekiah McCoy."

Fancy jumped up and walked swiftly over to Hezekiah and sat down next to him.

Khalil passed his sandwich, chips and soda to Eliana who gladly accepted it, and then he followed behind his mother.

When Hezekiah hung up the phone he relayed the news to Fancy and Khalil.

"They said he made it through surgery. They set his fractures, found where he was bleeding internally, and were able to stop it. He's headed to recovery and then to CCU, the critical care unit. The doctor said he'll come talk to us as soon as he can. The next twenty-four hours are critical though. But thank, God, he made it through surgery."

"Yes, thank you, God," Fancy said, not able to hold back her tears. "My baby, I want to see him so bad."

"You will, Ma."

She looked at Hezekiah. "Do you know what happened, Hezekiah?"

"Benny and I, believe it or not, rode up on the accident right after it happened. We heard a loud boom like an explosion. I didn't know what it was, but then traffic came to a complete halt. That's when we saw folks up ahead jumping out of their cars. It took almost an hour before traffic started moving again. Even then it was still at a snail's pace. When we finally made it up to the scene, there was an ambulance and fire truck. That's when I spotted the car. When I saw it, I told Benny it looked like the same kind of car Xavier drove. Benny pulled into a store parking lot and ran across the street and over to the accident scene to see if he could get a closer look. He came back and told me he saw them pulling the person out with the Jaws of Life. When they put him on the stretcher, he could clearly see it was Xavier. From what I can tell, it looked like he lost control of his car and hit one of those concrete construction embankments."

The doctor appeared and took them into another smaller room adjacent to the waiting room where he could talk to them privately.

Fancy listened as did Hezekiah. It was hard, if not impossible, to tell that the two of them had been what could only be described as mortal enemies. But the love of Xavier and his well-being had reunited them, if only for brief time.

"Your son," the doctor said, should have died from the impact of the crash alone. It's nothing short of a miracle that he survived. He sustained a head injury and facial and pelvic fractures but it's still a miracle he's alive. His prognosis remains guarded. He'll remain in critical care for the next few days."

"Can I see him?" Fancy asked.

"He's still heavily sedated, but I'll allow you to visit with him for five minutes. Then I'm going to ask you to allow him to rest. He has a slow recovery ahead."

"Thank you, doctor," Hezekiah spoke up. "God bless you."

"Yes, thank you," Khalil said and walked up to the doctor, extended his hand and they shook.

20

"If you kick a stone in anger, you'll hurt your own foot." Proverb

Khalil walked out of the hospital in the wee hours of the morning after having been there since early the day before. Fancy and Eliana were next to him. He was thankful at that moment for family but especially thankful his li'l brother survived what had been described to him as a horrendous, life threatening crash. As for his father, words couldn't express his feelings about his hospital appearance. On one hand it was good to see his father finally show some concern for his family, but Khalil couldn't help but think if this was another one of his father's ploys to wreak havoc and confusion. He didn't know which it was but he was confident that time would tell Hezekiah McCoy's true motives.

Hezekiah, Benny, and Isabella were drained. It had been a long 24 hours but there was little time for rest. They had to get back to the task at hand, getting Isabella to rehab.

Isabella's little boy rested in the back seat next to her, fast asleep.

"We'll get on the road after we go home, shower, and eat a good meal," Hezekiah told her. "I hope this deterrence hasn't caused you to change your mind. You know it's the best thing for you and for your kid." He looked in the back seat at Isabella and the boy.

Isabella listened in silence. She replayed the scene of the accident in her head. Benny and Hezekiah had been on the way to take her to rehab when they came upon the crash. When Benny told Hezekiah it was his son who was involved in the crash, taking her to rehab was the last thing on his mind. She couldn't blame him.

"I still want to go," Isabella told him. I know you've shelled out a lot of money to send me there."

"It's not about the money. This is your chance to make something out of your life."

Isabella would be in rehab for six months. Arrangements had been made, paperwork signed, and the knowledge that her child would be housed on the same grounds of the rehab facility, gave her renewed hope and confidence that maybe her life could turn around just as Hezekiah said.

Isabella hadn't prayed in a very long time. Her family life and her past hadn't exactly been one that included God. If anything, it was quite the opposite. The abuse and neglect at the hands of her mother was what prompted her to run away and never look back. She and her little brother were never taught about God. That's why when she met Hezekiah and his team as a homeless sixteen year old prostitute she was cautious and didn't entertain what they told her about God and how he would forgive her for all the things she'd done. When she was shown so much love and kindness by Hezekiah and some of the other Holy Rock Street Team members she began to have a glimmer of hope. That quickly changed when the relationship with Hezekiah turned sexual. He was no better than the other tricks she'd welcomed in and out of her bed and her life. Now, for some reason, because of Hezekiah's offer and suggestion she go into rehab, she began to believe maybe there was something to this God thing. Yes, he'd taken advantage of her, used her sexually, and fed her addiction, but he'd also provided a place for her and her son. A much safer place than being on the streets of Memphis.

Pepper knocked then pounded on Xavier's door repeatedly until someone next door opened their door and looked out. When the guy saw her, he frowned, showing his discontent with her incessant knocking.

"Uh, obviously no one's at home or they don't want to be bothered at two o'clock in the morning," the guy said, rubbing his eyes and sounding aggravated.

Pepper showed him a finger sign. "Screw you," she mouthed and then stormed down the stairs. She looked up and down the parking lot to see if she saw Xavier's car. She didn't. Standing in the dark, she called him again. It went to his voicemail. She texted him but there was no reply.

"Dang, I wish I had Ian's number. I bet you're somewhere hanging out with him. Why won't he stay out of our relationship and leave you alone. Ughh." Should she go to Ian's crib? It was in the same complex but she didn't know exactly which building nor his address. *Maybe I should drive through the complex and see if I see Xavier's or Ian's cars.*

As she walked toward her car, fighting to walk against the strong wind, she saw Eliana's car as it made the turn into the apartment complex and down Xavier's street.

Before she could flag her down, Eliana drove up and stopped behind Pepper's car.

"Eliana."

"Pepper, what are you doing out here at this time of morning?"

"Looking for Xavier. I'm worried about him. It's not like him not to return my calls or texts. Do you know if he's with your brother?" Pepper's hair and clothes blew against the high winds and her thin, shapely frame swayed from side to side.

"Get in the car," Eliana replied.

Pepper opened the passenger car door and got inside Eliana's car. "Look, I'm not trying to stir up drama, I just want to know if you've seen your brother and Xavier. That's it."

"Pepper, Xavier was in a car accident. He's in critical condition. I've been at the hospital with Pastor Khalil."

Pepper was floored. Xavier? In the hospital in critical condition? This couldn't be happening. Maybe she wasn't hearing her right.

"What did you say?"

"I *said*, Xavier is in the hospital. That's where I'm coming from. I just dropped Pastor Khalil and Sista McCoy off at home."

"You say he's in critical condition?" Her hand flew over her mouth and tears spouted from her eyes like a running faucet. "Oh, my God. I knew it was a reason he wasn't calling me back or responding to my text messages. What hospital? How is he?"

"Regional One. They're not letting anyone see him right now, except his immediate family, but even they weren't allowed to visit but five minutes."

Pepper broke down and boo-hooed.

Eliana reached around her shoulder and patted her on the back.

"It's going to be all right, Pepper. Remember, God is in control. We're just thankful that he survived. It could have been worse, you know. Why don't you go home. It's almost three o'clock in the morning. You do not need to be out here by yourself. Plus, it's about to storm."

Pepper continued crying but nodded as if she was in agreement with Eliana.

A boom of thunder sounded in the sky, confirming what Eliana said.

Pepper got out of Eliana's car. "Thanks, Eliana," she said between sobs.

"Get it together before you start driving, Pepper. We don't need another accident. Oh, wait. What's your phone number? I'll call you now and you can save my number. Call or text me to let me know you made it home safely."

"I will."

At home, Fancy undressed and climbed in the bed but sleep escaped her. Her mind was troubled, filled with concern for her son. She got out of her bed, went down on her knees, and began to pray and cry as the storm outside began delivering pounding rain crashing against her windowpane. The wind roared and thunder clashed.

When she finished praying and got off her knees, a bolt of lightning lit up the window, and Fancy jumped. Climbing underneath the bedcovers, she began to think about Hezekiah and how he showed up at the hospital. Sometimes the worst of times brings out the best in people.

The Hezekiah she saw at the hospital reminded her of the Hezekiah she first fell in love with. That Hezekiah was the type of man who loved and adored his family, who lavished her with gifts, who would do any and everything to keep his family happy. That Hezekiah was kind, always a hustler, and a man who genuinely loved God. What she wouldn't give to have that Hezekiah back.

21

"Of all the liars in the world, sometimes the worst are our own fears." Rudyard Kipling

"Fancy, how's Xavier?" Stiles asked.

"He's hanging in there. We didn't get home from the hospital until a few hours ago. I'm still in the bed. I haven't been able to sleep."

"I'm not going to keep you. I want you to know that I'm praying for him."

"How did you find out? You must have talked to Khalil."

"No, I haven't talked to him. I was going to call him after I finished talking to you. But to answer your question, I actually got a call not too long ago from Sista Mavis."

Fancy shook her head. "That woman is a walking news reporter. She just doesn't have a journalism degree and she isn't on television."

"Yea, she's a character. But in this case, I'm glad she called. I want to know what's going on in my family, you know. But enough talking; you try to get some rest."

"I don't know about that. I'm going to get up in an hour or so and head back to the hospital. I need to be by my son's side."

"I know you do, but just take care of yourself. Xavier is in good hands. The good Lord is going to bring him through this."

"I know he can and I know he will. Thank you."

"Keep me updated as often as you can. I'm going to call Khalil to see if he needs me to come fill in for him so he can have time to be with his brother."

"That would be good, but we don't want to take you away from your church every time Khalil is absent from the pulpit. There are some capable ministers on staff that can preach if that's what's needed."

"I understand that, but it's also the reason he brought me back as associate pastor. It's my duty to fill in for him when he's unavailable or having an emergency. This constitutes as an emergency, wouldn't you say?"

"Yes, absolutely. Well, whatever you and Khalil decide. It's not like y'all would listen to me anyway." Fancy grinned for the first time since she'd heard about her son.

Stiles laughed. "I wouldn't say all that. Anyway, I'm going to let you off this phone so you can rest. Keep me updated."

"Okay, I will. Goodbye, Stiles and thanks for calling."

"No problem. See ya." Stiles ended the call.

Listening to Pandora through her Bose Bluetooth speaker, Detria danced around the sitting room, totally dismissing the raging thunderstorm outside.

Priscilla walked into the entrance of the room and stood with hands on hips, smiling and shaking her head at the sight of seeing Detria dancing and hearing the music blasting.

Detria danced until she looked over toward the door and saw Priscilla standing in the doorway with a big grin.

"What has you so happy this morning?"

Pausing the music, she asked. "Did you say something, Priscilla?

"Yes, I said what has you dancing around like a teeny bopper on this stormy morning?"

"Oh, I'm just feeling good. It's a brand new day, Priscilla." The effects of the powder sometimes made her giddy and hyper. "Things are about to change for the better. You're going to see a new me."

Priscilla tilted her head slightly. "Ohhh, is that right? How so?"

"You'll see. Just believe me when I tell you that from here on out, it's all about me, Priscilla." Detria laughed, took the music off PAUSE and started dancing again.

"Okay, then. Do you want me to make you some breakfast?"

"What did you say?"

Priscilla repeated herself, speaking louder to make her voice carry over the music.

Detria bobbed her head and kept on doing her moves until the song ended. She turned the music off and followed the aroma coming from the kitchen.

"Smells good. You know you can burn, Priscilla."

"Girl, what's got you in such a good mood?"

"I told you, it's a new me."

"I hope that's a good thing. You know I want what's best for you. And I sure hope this new you means you're going to start spending time with Elijah. Your son needs you."

"I know, but he doesn't like to be around me. You know that, Priscilla."

"That's because he senses you feel the same way about him. If you start spending more time with him, calling him more, and just letting him know you love him, then you'd be surprised at how quickly he'll want to be with you."

"Maybe so. I'll have to think on that one, but at least I'm going to start working on me. I'm going to even start going to church more often."

Priscilla paused momentarily from mixing the bacon and cheese omelet to look at Detria. "Say what?"

"Yep, I sure am."

"Are you going to go to church with me?"

"Sure, why not. And I'm going to go with my sister and her family too. I miss hanging out with Brooke."

"I'm sure she misses you, too. You girls used to be so close a few years back."

"I know, but I had my own problems and she has her own family. You know I'm not one to intrude on other people and what they have going on."

"She's not other people; she's your one and only sister. There's nothing like family. I wish I still had my family."

"I thought I was your family."

"Of course you are, but you know what I mean."

Priscilla poured the omelet mix into the skillet and then popped wheat bread into the toaster.

"No pancakes?"

"You were so busy dancing, you never said whether you wanted pancakes or not. I can still make up a batch. It won't take but a minute."

Detria raised a hand to stop her. "No, omelet and toast will be more than enough. I've danced so much I've worked up an appetite."

"I'm glad to hear that. You eat like a bird sometimes. But we both know why that is."

Detria's smile faded. "Let's not go there, Priscilla."

"I'm just saying, I wish you would stop using that stuff. It'll be the death of you."

"I said I'm going to stop messing with it, at least not as much as I used to."

Priscilla looked over her shoulder at Detria.

"At least I'm not lying to your face. I said I'm going to ease up on it and that's what I mean."

"Thank God for that. Well, anyway, on another note, that's a shame about Pastor Khalil's brother isn't it? Any word on how he's doing?"

"Who? What are you talking about?"

"Didn't you see it on your phone? You read everything on that phone. I can't believe you haven't seen that. The boy was in a car accident on Winchester where they're doing all that construction. He's in critical condition. That's what the news said, but you know how they get stuff messed up."

Detria went to her news app and opened it. There were several stories, mostly about crimes that had occurred overnight. She scrolled pass the stories until she came up on the one about Xavier. She read the story and immediately texted Khalil. Without waiting on a response, she dialed his number but it went to his voicemail.

"Dang. I can't believe you're just saying something about this."

"I thought you knew."

"No, but I'm sure going to find out what happened."

She shot Khalil another text. When he didn't answer that one she called Holy Rock. Sista Mavis mouth of the south answered.

"Good morning, Holy Rock Ministries."

"Khalil please," Detria announced, not bothering to address him by his title.

"And who is this?" Sista Mavis asked.

"Is he in the office?"

"And I asked, who's calling?" Sista Mavis knew that voice. It was like a parent being able to pick out their kid from a thousand other kids in a crowd. "He's not available. How may I help you?"

"You can't help me. Is that what's her name, his administrative assistant in the office?"

"No, she isn't. What can I do for you?"

"Sista Mavis, the only thing you can do for me is tell me what's going on with Xavier. I know you know the full four-one-one. I mean, you do know everything about everything. Don't you?" Detria snapped, purposely allowing sarcasm to drip from her mouth like sorghum syrup.

"May I take a message?"

"Yes, you sure can. This is Detria Graham, but you already know that, Sista Mavis."

"And?" Sista Mavis shot back.

"And don't mess with me, ol' lady. You should know I don't play."

"I wouldn't exactly say that. You play a lot, play around these Godly men, enticing 'em into your wicked bed. You're nothing but a modern day Delilah, a harlot, a Jezebel. Now, if you don't want to leave a message for Pastor Khalil, I'm going to end this call. Unlike some folks, I have to work for a living."

"Awwww, you poor thing." A curse word or two trailed out of her mouth. Detria ended the call first. Sista Mavis could make her so mad.

Going to her bedroom, she called Khalil again. Same thing. Voicemail. Texted him. Still no response.

The next number she dialed she got an answer.

"What do you want? I thought I told you to stay out of my life."

"Good morning to you, too. I thought you might want to know that your baby boy is laying in a hospital bed. Word is he was in some kind of car accident. S'pose to be pretty messed up."

"What makes you think I don't know what's going on with my son? I'm not going to tell you this again, Detria, stay out of my business and don't you go near that hospital."

"You know what, screw you, Hezekiah! I don't care what happens to that punk, and I sure as heck don't care what happens to you. I hope they lock your behind up for the next twenty years!"

Hezekiah burst into boisterous laughter and ended the call.

161

22

*"To us, family means putting your arms around
each other and being there."*
Barbara Bush

*P*epper tossed and turned throughout the night. It was early morning, and as her eyes opened, she struggled to get out of bed. Feeling the effects of having had little if any sleep, there was no way she would be productive at work today so she made the quick decision to call in sick. Granted, she knew she would face her mother's mouth. Victoria had excellent work ethics, which is why she had accumulated a boatload of vacation, sick, and PTO hours. Pepper was not her mother, and no matter how many times she told Victoria that, Victoria didn't want to hear it. It was the main reason Pepper regretted accepting the position working at the same company as her mom.

Her supervisor's administrative assistant answered the phone. "Good morning, HR."

"Good morning, Melinda." Pepper changed her voice from her normal squeaky voice to a coarse one, complete with a cough here and there. "I won't be in today. I have a bug or something." She coughed again.

"Okay, I'll let Mr. Ammons know." Melinda sounded like she wasn't too convinced, but what could she say or do? It wasn't her business. She was the messenger and having worked in the HR department for ten years, she learned not to get bent out of shape over other people's issues and problems. One thing she *did* know was Pepper Rawlings was probably not going to last as an employee of the The Baker Group. Young people like her often took their jobs for granted. They would stay a while and then quit or get fired. Because Victoria Rawlings' was a model employee, and all around smart woman with a great personality, and excellent work ethics, Pepper would probably be given a little leeway. Yet, knowing Victoria the way she believed she knew her, Melinda figured she would light into her daughter if word got out she was missing excessive time from work.

"Hope you feel better."

"Thanks, Melinda."

Too early to go to the hospital. I'll get me a couple hours more sleep and then get up and go see about my man. Pepper crawled back into the bed, turned on her left side, and went back to sleep.

Fancy arrived at the hospital and found Khalil already there in the CCU waiting area. "Why didn't you call and let me know you were coming?"

"I wanted you to get some rest. I was going to call you a little later and let you know how Xavier was doing."

"I'm his mother, and yours too. You know I am not going to sit around at home and wait on you, this hospital, or anyone else to call me to tell me about my son."

Khalil stood up and hugged his mother. "Ma, I wasn't trying to do that. You know I love you. I just thought I'd run up here, check on him before I went to Holy Rock. That's all. I know wild bulls couldn't keep you from this hospital as long as one of your children was in here."

Fancy's mood softened. "Have you seen the doctor?"

"Not yet. The nurse said he should be making his rounds in about an hour."

"Have they let you see Xavier?"

Khalil looked at his phone. "We should be able to go in to see him at 8:30."

"Okay, good. Just another ten minutes."

"But, Ma, you know we can only stay for five minutes."

"Yea, I know. Five minutes every three hours. I don't care if I'm in there for one minute, I just want my baby to know that I'm here."

Khalil's text notifier sounded, and immediately in mid conversation with Fancy, he showed his frustration. "Dang, this girl is crazee."

"Who?"

"Dee. She keeps blowing my phone up. Been texting and calling me like she mad since my feet hit the floor."

Fancy shook her head. "It's easy to get mixed up with those kind of women, but it's hell to get rid of 'em. I hope you've learned your lesson and realize that those kinda women are only good for one thing and they can only bring you down, son."

"I know, Ma. I'm done with her. She's texting me about Xavier."

"How does she know about Xavier? Oh, I guess your father told her."

"Yea, probably. Either way, I'm about to block her."

"Good for you. Now what about Eliana.?

"What do you mean?"

"You know what I mean. Do you like her? She's a nice girl."

"She a'ite, but she's my personal assistant, Ma. That's it."

"Boy, please. Who do you think you're talking to? It's plain as day that the two of you have something going on. I don't know how far it's gone, but a blind man can see that she likes you, and I think you like her too."

Khalil blushed. "Come on, Ma. It's time to go see Xavier."

Fancy looped her arm into her son's. She wasn't finished with the conversation, but she'd done exactly what she intended—open the door that could lead to revealing if Khalil had feelings for Eliana. Seeing how Eliana stuck by him last night endeared her to the girl even more. Initially, when Fancy introduced Eliana to Holy Rock and Khalil, Fancy had ideas in the back of her mind about a match between her and Khalil. But when her brother came into the picture and tried to stake his claim on Xavier, Fancy backed away from Eliana. She didn't want or need Ian in her son's life. As she gave it some thought, Fancy reasoned Eliana could be the one to convince her brother to back off Xavier. Fast forward, Pepper. When Victoria's daughter moved to Memphis it was a godsend, an answer to Fancy's prayers when it came to her baby. Fancy explained to Victoria and Pepper about her son being pursued by a gay man, Ian. Fancy was totally against that. Pepper didn't have to be told anything else. At Fancy's divorce party, Pepper showed what she was made of. She had the power to change Fancy's gay son straight and that was the nail in the coffin. Now Fancy could concentrate on getting her sons married. Khalil to Eliana. Xavier to Pepper.

Fancy and Khalil stood on the side of Xavier's bed. He looked nothing like the handsome young man he was before the horrifying accident. Fancy fought back tears.

"Baby, I'm here. Mama's here," she assured Xavier as she took hold of his swollen hand.

"I'm here, too, bruh. You're going to pull through this. Everything is going to be fine."

Xavier heard his mother and brother. Where was he and why couldn't he open his eyes and see them? It was like he was in a dream state, floating around the universe, hovering over sites, places, and seeing people he hadn't seen since he was a kid. Why was his brother telling him he was going to be fine and his mother saying she was here. Where was *here*? He was confused but he didn't feel upset or frightened, nothing like that. Quite the opposite. He felt peaceful, light as a feather, with no cares in the world.

"We'll be back at the next visiting hour, sweetheart. You rest and get better. The whole church is praying for you."

"Yeah, man. You even got your dad to come see you. Now that's an achievement in and of itself. You know." Khalil laughed and squeezed his brother's other hand from the opposite side of the bed. "We got to leave, but like Ma said, we'll be back. Love you, man."

I love you, too, Khalil. Xavier questioned himself. *Did he hear me?*

Fancy leaned over and kissed her baby boy. "I love you, baby. I'll be back soon." A tear fell on Xavier's face and rolled down.

Xavier felt a soft as cotton touch on the side of his face, followed by a slight moistness. *I love you back, Ma. Don't worry about a thing, Ma. I'm good. I really am.*

Khalil embraced his mother as they walked out of the CCU and headed back toward the waiting room. Opening the door for his mother, she walked ahead. There were several more people gathered in the waiting room, much more than when they first left.

Khalil followed Fancy as she took a seat midway the room and close to the television and coffee machine.

"Do you want to go downstairs and have some breakfast before I leave?"

"No, I'm going to make myself a cup of coffee, watch Good Morning America, and scroll on social media. You go on to Holy Rock. Take care of your business."

"You sure?"

"Yes. Oh, son, did you talk to Stiles?"

"Yes. I talked to him yesterday."

"Is he coming back to help out while Xavier's in the hospital?"

"I told him it was up to him. I still plan on preaching every Sunday, but maybe not at all three services so if he wants to and it won't interfere with his obligations to Full of Grace, then I'd welcome him to come back. At least for a few weeks."

Fancy's scowl turned into a relaxed look as she exhaled. "That would be good for you, for Holy Rock, for all of us. It would take pressure off of you until Xavier gets better."

"Good morning."

Fancy looked pass Khalil. Khalil looked over his shoulder.

"Pepper? Sweetheart, it's good to see you here," Fancy said and stood up and hugged the girl.

Pepper was glad she'd called in sick. To see how pleased Fancy was to see her made her feel like everything was falling into place.

"Hi, Pepper."

"Hi, Pastor Khalil. Uh, how is Xavier? I was so upset when Eliana told me he'd been involved in a car accident."

"We just saw him. They're only allowing immediate family to see him, and then it's only five minutes every three hours."

"I understand, but I'm here for the two of you."

"Come on, sit down." Fancy urged and walked back over to her chair and sat down. She pat the chair next to her and Pepper sat down.

"Well, Ma, I'm going to head to Holy Rock. I'll be back in time for the next visitation hour, but if you need me before then, give me a call."

Fancy looped her arm into Pepper's. "I'll be fine. Pepper's here to keep me company. Right, sweetheart?"

"Yes, ma'am. I don't plan on going anywhere. Have you had breakfast? We can go to the hospital cafeteria and see what they have to offer."

"Yes, sure," Fancy said.

Khalil laughed, seeing the pleased look on his mother's face. He leaned down and kissed her on the cheek. "I'll see you later."

"Bye, son. Oh, and don't think I've forgotten that conversation. We'll going to finish it."

"I know we will, Ma." Khalil smiled knowingly and walked away.

Moments after Khalil left, Fancy and Pepper went to find the cafeteria. Once there, they placed their orders and spent the next hour laughing and talking. Fancy shared stories with Pepper about Xavier when he was a little boy and a teen. It felt good to have a girl like Pepper interested in her son.

The conversation turned serious when Pepper took the chance to confess to Fancy how she felt about Xavier.

"I love him, Mrs. McCoy. I don't know how you feel about me telling you this, but I had this compelling desire to tell you."

Fancy reached across the small table and placed her long, beautifully polished nails on top of Pepper's hand. "Honey, that's the best news I've heard in a long time."

Pepper smiled big. Was she hearing Fancy right? Did she say this was the best news she'd heard in a long time? Boy was she glad she'd taken off work and came to the hospital. With Fancy in her corner, when Xavier got better things could really take off for the two of them. Ian wouldn't stand a chance.

"You're happy?"

"Happy? Pepper, you're my best friend's daughter. You're like her in so many ways. You've been good for Xavier ever since the first day I introduced the two of you. Victoria called it right. She told me you and Xavier would make the perfect couple, and she was right. But, listen, between you and me, you know there's still one small problem."

Pepper squinted and eased her hand from underneath Fancy's hand. "What's that?"

"It's not what, it's who. That boy—Ian."

Pepper nodded in agreement. "Don't worry. I'm already on it. I have to make Xavier see that Ian is not who he wants."

"Yes. See, that's why I like you, Pepper. We're on one accord."

Pepper was feeling herself. The morning had turned out way better than she could ever have anticipated. Yes, Xavier was still in bad shape, but she believed with each day he would improve and eventually his wounds would heal. Until that time, and while he was in the hospital, she and Fancy agreed she would be by his side at every opportunity once he was allowed to have other visitors besides family.

"I'm going to talk to the doctor and explain you are an important part of Xavier's life and you would be good for his recovery. I'll let him know you're just like family."

"Would you do that?"

The elevator dinged and they stepped inside. They dispensed of their conversation until the two people on the elevator got off on the next floor.

"Of course I would do that. I mean, it's not really a lie. You *are* like family. I don't see it being a problem."

"Thank you so much."

The elevator arrived to their designated floor. The ladies stepped off and continued talking as they walked.

Pepper noticed a familiar person walking toward them as they neared the CCU Waiting Room.

"Look, it's Ian."

Fancy's face turned into a mass of fury as Ian approached.

"Pepper? Mrs. McCoy. My sister told me about Xavier. How is he? Can I see him?"

Fancy rolled her eyes. "What are you doing here? Only immediate family is allowed."

Ian eyed Pepper. "Then what are you doing here?" he bit back.

"That's none of your concern," Fancy spoke up.

"Please, I just want to know how he is."

Fancy softened her attitude. "He has a long way to go, but I know God is a healer. My boy will be fine as long as he knows he's surrounded by his family and those who love him," looping her arm inside of Pepper's.

Ian glanced at the show of solidarity between the two ladies and knew instantaneously that he had no chance of getting near Xavier, not while Xavier was in the hospital, at least.

"I understand, and that's why I'm here. I want him to know that I'm praying for him and that I love him."

Fancy stepped up on Ian and gritted her teeth. "Let me tell you something, and I don't want to tell you this again. Leave my son alone! Stay away from this hospital, you little twit."

Ian was livid. "I don't think you can make me stay away. You don't own this place. I can come and go as I please."

"You very well might be right about that, but I do have control over who sees my son and who's good for my son. And you better know that when I finish talking to his doctors and this staff, they'll keep you as far away from my son and this hospital, too. I'll have you locked up if you try to see him, if you so much as ask about him. Do you understand me?" Fancy pointed her finger into his face as she bared her teeth like a pit bull ready to attack.

Ian fake smiled. "Yea, I hear you, *First Lady*. I hear you loud and clear." He smirked at Pepper and then turned and walked back in the direction he came.

"Come on, let's go, sweetheart," Fancy told Pepper and they continued toward the CCU Waiting Room.

23

"The greatest healing therapy is friendship and love." Hubert H. Humphrey

Khalil entered through the doors of Holy Rock and was greeted by staff members telling him that Xavier and the McCoy family were in their prayers. Some hugged him, others shook his hand, patted his back, and reassured him about the goodness of God, and so on.

Sista Mavis came from around her desk and out of her work area, approaching Khalil in the hallway.

"Pastor K, how is he?"

"He's going to be just fine, Sista Mavis. God is able."

"Oh, yes, he is. I've been praying all night for that boy. You young folk drive so fast. You have to be careful, look out for these other drivers."

"Thank you for your prayers, Sista Mavis."

Sista Mavis returned to her area and had a seat, but her eyes remained glued on Khalil. She watched as his eyes locked in on Eliana's vacant chair. He quickly scanned the office space where she and the other admins sat but he didn't see her.

"If you're wondering about Sista Eliana, she won't be in until noon. I thought she would have told you," Sista Mavis fished.

"Oh, that's right. I forgot. Thanks, Sista Mavis."

"If I can help you with something, let me know. I have access to your calendar."

"Will you contact Pastor Graham for me, Sista Mavis. Call in my office when you have him on the phone."

"I sure will."

"Oh, if I get any calls pertaining to my brother, put them through. No, wait, let me clarify that. If I get any calls from the hospital about my brother, put them through. Anyone else, take a message or send them to my office voicemail. One more thing, make sure the Youth Department staff is made aware that my brother will be out until further notice. When Eliana comes in I'll get her to write an official memo but if you'll do that for me, that should be sufficient for now."

"Yes, Pastor K. I'll get right on it."

Khalil disappeared up the hallway and entered his office.

Shortly thereafter, after having sat down, powered on his desktop, his interoffice phone rang. "Pastor Graham is on line two," Sista Mavis told him.

"Good morning, Stiles."

"Good morning. How's Xavier?"

"I just came from the hospital. He's still on a ventilator, and he's not conscious. They have him heavily sedated for now, and he's still in critical condition. Thanks for asking."

"Well, I have him on our prayer list. We have prayer warriors who pray every Tuesday at noon. Plus, I'm praying every day. How are you?"

"I'm good. Tired. I haven't been able to get any real rest, but it's all good. You know you do what you have to do when it comes to family and when it comes to the church."

"True. True."

"I wanted to know if you could possibly fill in for me for a few weeks."

"I'm sure I can. I'll get things arranged here for my absence. If you can give me a few days, I should be able to be there by the weekend."

"Straight. I appreciate it."

Stiles laughed. "That's what you're paying me the big bucks for."

"I guess you have a point. I'll see you in a few days."

"Okay, nephew. I'll let you know my flight information as soon as I have it."

"Thanks. Have a good one."

"You too. Keep the faith, man. Xavier is going to be all right. How is Fancy?"

"I left her at the hospital. You know it's going to be like pulling teeth to get her away from there. That's another reason I need you here. With you in the office, I won't have to be as concerned about what's going on. I know I have capable staff, but Hezekiah McCoy makes it hard for me to fully trust and rely on them. I never know who he might have on his private payroll. Know what I mean?"

"I hope it's not like that. He's already facing prison time. And from what Fancy told me, he was at the hospital before either of you. God must be dealing with him."

"Yeah, maybe. But you know, time will tell. Anyway, I'm out. See you this weekend."

"You bet."

Feeling relieved that Stiles would be returning, Khalil focused his attention on working on his sermon when his cell phone rang. He looked at the screen. It was Detria again. He started to answer it but decided not to. He was done with her for good this time. She'd served her purpose. He didn't care why she pretended to be so interested in the welfare of his brother. The phone call was followed by another text message. Enough was enough. He did like he told his mother he was going to do. He blocked her number, exhaled, and returned to working on his message.

A knock on his door interrupted him this time. He was quickly becoming frustrated. "Yes, come in."

It was Sista Mavis. "Pastor K, I'm sorry to bother you, but Detria Graham is calling this office like a mad woman. I keep telling her you aren't available but she keeps calling me a liar. I've sent her to your voicemail, which is going to be full before you know it with all the calling she's doing. I don't know what to do. I'm trying to behave like the Christian woman I am, but enough is enough. That woman has a problem. She seriously needs God in her life."

"Calm down, Sista Mavis. If she calls again, send the call through the next time. But if she comes to this church, I want you to call security immediately. Do you understand?"

"Yes, Pastor K."

"Okay, now please close my door. I'm working on my message."

Sista Mavis closed the door and returned to her desk. Sure enough within five minutes of her leaving, she buzzed his office and told him Detria was on the phone.

"Look, what is wrong with you? I said leave me the hell alone. Do you understand me?"

"Khalil, please, all I want is to see how Xavier is doing. I heard about his accident. Someone said he was dead."

"I'm going to tell you this this one last time. So you listen, and you betta listen good, Dee. My family is no concern of yours. Now for the final time, do not call me ever again. Not on my phone, not at Holy Rock, and if you see me on the street you'll be smart to cross to the other side."

Detria lost it and began cussing and screaming. "You used me, Khalil McCoy. You and your no good daddy are just alike. But you're going to pay. You watch what I tell you."

"I'm going to say it again, if I even so much as hear or see you near me or my family ever again, you won't live to see another day or snort another line." Khalil hung up the phone, mumbled under his breath, "Crazy wanch," and returned to working on his message.

"Ian, I'll let you know how Xavier is doing. Just promise me you'll stay away from the hospital and from Khalil's family."

Eliana had gone with her brother for his follow-up doctor's appointment because of an HIV scare. "That's easy for you to say when you're all up on Khalil. My friend is in the hospital and you don't want me to be concerned about him?"

"I didn't say anything like that, Ian, and you know it."

"How is he, Eliana?"

"He's got a long road to recovery is all I can say. I mean he ran head on into a concrete embankment. Thank God he's alive."

Ian thought back to when he learned the accident happened. It was the same evening Xavier left his apartment in a messed up state of mind. Xavier was no drinker, so the shots of tequila he drank had added to his erratic behavior. Ian's plan for him to spend the night backfired as the conversation about Leo's murder escalated. If only he could somehow have kept him from barging out the apartment and climbing behind the wheel, Xavier wouldn't be laying up in a hospital bed near death.

"You don't understand, Eliana, I need to see him. You have to help me. Please."

Eliana looked at her brother. "Help you? I won't help you sneak into the hospital to see Xavier, if that's what you're talking about. I can't even see him. Only immediate family. Just pray for him, Ian. That's all you or I can do right now."

Ian rubbed his head back and forth and began to cry as he went round and round. "Oh, God, this is my fault. This is all my fault."

Eliana's brows furrowed as she went over to her brother and grabbed both of his shoulders so he faced her. "What are you talking about? How can Xavier's accident be your fault?"

Ian thought about what he was saying. "It is. Xavier is so confused about his life. I told him over and over again to be who he is."

"You mean, gay?"

"Yes," Ian said and nodded. "But he couldn't deal with it. The night of the accident, we had a big blowout about it. He was talking about that skank, Pepper and being with her, but I was pressuring him to be with me. He ended up leaving in a bad state of mind. When you told me about the evening he had the accident, it was the same evening we argued." Tears poured. What Ian said was true, but he hadn't told Eliana about the rest of the conversation regarding Leo, and he wasn't going to tell her either. No one could know about that.

"That doesn't make it your fault, Ian." Eliana wrapped her arms around her brother and hugged him tightly. "It's not your fault. Don't do this to yourself. We just got good news at your doctor's visit. You don't have HIV. You should be celebrating right now about God's goodness. That false positive could have come out totally different." She held him and allowed him to cry on her shoulder until he was spent.

Ian was glad the latest round of tests confirmed he did not have the disease but he did have a treatable auto immune disease. She pulled back and they looked at each other. "I have to get to work. I'm supposed to be there by noon. I want you to stay here, at my apartment, and chill. I'll check on you later. Okay?"

Ian nodded and wiped his eyes with the back of his hand.

"I promise to tell you whatever I find out about Xavier."

"Thanks, sis."

"I love you, Ian. There's nothing I wouldn't do to protect you. You know that, don't you?" She kissed him on his cheek.

"Yes," he said, barely audible.

Eliana turned and left.

24

*"Nature performs the cure, the physician takes
the fee." Benjamin Franklin*

*S*tiles preached a soul stirring message at Full of Grace. He loved Full of Grace, was grateful for the opportunity to pastor the six hundred member congregation, but Holy Rock was and still remained at the forefront of his heart. He could understand now as a man, and a pastor, how endearing Holy Rock was to him, the same as it was to Pastor.

Finishing his packing at home later that evening, he reminisced about the good times and not so good times he had at Holy Rock, starting when he was a little boy up to when he was appointed to be senior pastor. And like a little kid, he felt the nervousness and excitement of knowing he was going back to Holy Rock, if only for a few weeks.

The following Monday morning, Stiles got out of bed, eager for his trip. What he didn't like was the reason he was called to come to Holy Rock. His nephew was lying in a hospital bed in pretty bad shape. Stiles said a prayer for Xavier, then texted Kareena to let her know he was ready.

Kareena arrived twenty minutes later.

At the airport, Kareena steered her car into the farthest right lane and stopped in front of the airline terminal.

"Hold it down while I'm gone, Kareena, like you always do." Stiles looked over at her, laughed, and opened the car door. They did a fist bump and he got out of her car.

"Okay, have a safe trip. Talk to you later."

"Thanks. See you in a coupla weeks, Kareena." Stiles closed the front door, and walked to the back of Kareena's car. She popped the trunk and he removed his luggage, closed the trunk, and threw up his hand to her as he disappeared inside the busy terminal.

She watched a few seconds before driving off. Her phone rang. It was River.

"Hi, babe," she said, and a loving smile appeared on her face as she merged with the traffic exiting the airport.

"Eliana, who did you say is going to pick up my uncle?" Khalil asked while driving to the hospital.

"Brother Ron is on his way there now. No worries, Pastor Khalil. We have everything taken care of. After that, he's going to take Minister Stiles to his house so he can get settled in. You know, drop off his luggage, pick up his car, whatever he wants to do."

"Cool. Well, you know where I'm going to be."

"Yes, at the hospital. Please let Xavier know he remains in my prayers."

"I will. Thanks, Eliana."

"Is your mother with you?"

"Yes, she's right here." Khalil looked at his mother. "She can hear you."

"Good afternoon, First Lady."

"Hey, sweetheart. How are you?"

"I'm good. How are you?"

"I'm hanging in there. Thank you for making sure everything is running smoothly at Holy Rock so my son," she rubbed Khalil's arm, "can be with Xavier and with me. You don't know how much relief it gives me to have someone capable running that office and handling Khalil's administrative needs."

"That's what I'm here for."

"Well, you're a jewel." Fancy continued to build her up, hoping Khalil would take notice at what she was saying and how well she and Eliana were getting along lately. Maybe this would strengthen the relationship he had with Eliana.

"Thank you, First Lady."

"She's just speaking the truth, Eliana. You *are* one special lady. Anyway, I'll hit you back later. In the meantime, you know what to do when my uncle gets there. Make sure he has everything he needs."

"I'm on it."

"Okay, call you later." Khalil pressed the button on his steering wheel to end the call.

Fancy looked at him and smiled.

"What, Ma?"

"You know what."

"No, I don't know."

"Eliana is a good girl, Khalil."

"That she is."

"And you're a pastor now. A pastor of a growing church. I mean, Holy Rock and you are blasted on television stations all over the mid-south...and the U.S. Thousands upon thousands tune in to see and hear you preach on livestream. You're on the radio now. I mean, honey," she expressed, "people are beginning to recognize you on the streets. Even at the hospital. Think about how many people have stopped you to ask if you're Pastor Khalil McCoy. How many people have stopped you, and asked you to pray for them or their loved ones?"

"Ma, you're right but what does that have to do with Eliana?" Khalil shrugged and continued driving.

"You're twenty-four years old. You're handsome, successful, and smart, You're financially secure, and you're going to be making even more money as time goes by. You'll reach multi-millionaire status in no time, if you haven't already. You're well respected at Holy Rock and in the community, but you have one thing lacking."

"What's that, Ma?" he glanced at his mother.

"A first lady."

Khalil chuckled. "Ma, you got to be kidding me. A first lady?" he shook his head in disagreement. "Uhh, I don't think so."

"That's the problem. You need to start 'thinking so', son. These young hussies are all over you. How many times have your armor bearers had to get you out of the sanctuary at the end of each service before you get ran down with a deluge of young women wanting to get you into their beds? They all want to be the one that you'll put a ring on it." Fancy grinned at the thought. "They'll do whatever they can to wear the title of First Lady. You know I'm right."

Khalil laughed again. "Yea, sometimes it *can* get a little wild at Holy Rock."

"I know you're young and you don't want to settle down, but you're leading a different life now, sweetheart." She rubbed his shoulder again. "You're not that young wild, reckless, juvenile in Chicago anymore. I've watched you come into your own. For a man of twenty four, you're mature and wise beyond your years. Look at what you've done at Holy Rock, Khalil. You're the one responsible for the major growth of that church. People flock to Holy Rock all because of you...and God, of course. He's showing you so much favor, Khalil. You need a strong woman by your side. I know you've seen pictures and billboards, even visited and come to know some of the pastors who have their first lady standing right beside them. Some of those women are co-pastors with their husbands. I'm not saying Eliana will step into the role of being a co-pastor, then again who knows where God will lead her. What I *am* saying is you have a good girl right in front of your face. She's down for you. She's smart, she's wise, she's beautiful, she loves the Lord and she loves you."

Khalil did a goose neck stretch and looked over at his mother. "Loves me? I don't know about all of that."

"Believe me, a woman knows. And I know, without you telling me, you and her have been doing something outside of Holy Rock. You can deny it all you want, but you can't fool me, and *she* can't fool me. I see the way her face lights up every time your name is mentioned. I hear it in her voice over the phone when she talks about you. My mother always said to marry someone who loves you more than you love them."

Khalil's face grew serious.

Fancy could tell she had given him a reason to think seriously about what she'd said.

They arrived at the hospital. "I'm going to park. I'll meet you in the lobby, unless you want to head to CCU."

"No, I'll wait on you."

"Cool. I'll be back."

Fancy got out of the car, closed the door, and smiled as she strutted into the hospital. She knew her sons. All Eliana had to do was to keep doing what she was doing and she might just find herself walking down the aisle as Khalil's bride.

Standing inside the hospital entrance, Fancy took a second look at the gentleman standing in the corner of the entrance talking to another man. She took a step back to get a better look. The man looked like Winston. She hadn't seen or talked to him ever since she blocked his number.

Everything about their relationship, she wanted to forget. He had hurt her badly, had betrayed her, and if she never heard from him again it would be too soon.

The stranger shook the other man's hand, and turned to walk away. Fancy placed a hand over her chest and exhaled expecting to see him but when she got a full view of the man, he clearly wasn't Winston.

"You ready?" Khalil asked, interrupting her thoughts.

"Yes, let's go see my baby."

Arriving at the CCU, as required, they stopped and checked in at the nurses' station.

"Good afternoon, we're here to see Xavier McCoy."

"Good afternoon, Pastor McCoy. Hello, Mrs. McCoy," the pleasant nurse said. "I have good news."

Fancy's curiosity was peaked as was Khalil's.

"Mr. McCoy was transferred to a private room this morning."

Fancy was elated. "Thank you, Lord. Thank you, thank you, thank you." She raised both hands in praise.

Khalil smiled, grabbed his mother's hand as he looked upward. "Yes, thank you, God."

"Where is he?" Fancy asked.

"He's in, let me be sure," the nurse looked at the computer in front of her, entered something and then looked at Fancy and Khalil, "on the orthopedic floor, room 431."

"Thank you," Khalil told the burgundy-haired nurse, before turning and walking away.

Khalil and Fancy talked about how excited they were to be given the good news. It was a long walk, crooks and turns, following color coded hospital hallways. Two elevators later they arrived on the orthopedic floor.

"Here it is," Khalil told his mom, and pointed to room 431. He knocked lightly first before peaking his head inside the room.

He opened the door and he and his mother walked into the dark hospital room. Standing next to his bedside, Fancy became overcome with emotion.

Xavier's eyes were shut, tubes were still in his nose but it appeared he was off the ventilator.

"Xavier, can you hear me, baby?" Fancy rubbed his hand which remained swollen but not as swollen as it had been.

The doctor walked into the room. "Good morning."

"Hello, doctor," Khalil and Fancy replied respectively.

"I'm bet you're glad to see your son out of CCU."

Khalil nodded and Fancy responded by saying, "Yes, it is a blessing. How is he?"

The doctor examined Xavier, removed the chart from the end of his bed, and read over his notes, then called Xavier's name. Xavier didn't respond. He turned and focused on Fancy and Khalil. "We removed the ventilator last night and he did well. We're slowly taking him off some of the medication that has him sedated so you should see him opening his eyes soon and trying to communicate. But if he should wake up, I'd like you to encourage him to rest. I don't want him doing a lot of talking. Right now we still have pain medication being fed intravenously every four hours. When he's doing better and fully conscious, he'll be able to push the pain medication button himself."

"So has his prognosis changed?" Khalil inquired.

"He's been upgraded to serious. We won't know the extent of his head injury until he's fully awake. I can't say how bad it is or if there will be long term effects. When he first came into the trauma center, to be honest, we weren't expecting him to survive, but I guess someone must have been praying for him because he's made it this far."

Fancy teared up. "We're a praying family, doctor. My son here," she touched Khalil on his arm and looked at him, "is a pastor."

"Well, I'm a believer too, and I certainly believe in prayer and in the power of God to heal."

Fancy studied the doctor's name badge. She'd read it before but hadn't allowed it to register in her mind because so many doctors had worked on her son. But now, hearing he was a praying man, gave Fancy renewed hope and an even stronger faith.

"Thank you, Dr. Daniels. You don't know how much it means to hear you confess that you know the Lord."

"Yes, I do. I had a praying mother and grandmother. My father was a pastor before he died of cancer five years ago."

"God bless you, brother," Khalil said.

"Thank you. Well, let me continue my rounds. I'll be back tomorrow. Keep sending those prayers up for this young man." He patted Xavier's leg and then exited the room, but not before tilting his head and he and Fancy exchanging a lingering smile at one another.

"Thank you, we will, Dr. Daniels," Fancy said, again, still smiling while she sat down in the chair next to Xavier's bed.

25

"Be not wise in your own eyes; fear the Lord, and turn away from evil. It will be healing to your flesh and refreshment to your bones."
Proverbs 3:7-8

Stiles unpacked his suitcase, took a shower, and then went to the refrigerator to see what he could find to eat. He was pleased to find a fully stocked fridge and freezer. Opening some of the kitchen cabinets, there was a plethora of canned goods, spices, and cooking utensils. He was set. The only thing is he wasn't in the frame of mind to cook just yet. He wanted to get to Holy Rock as soon as he could so he opted to leave the cooking to later. He would stop along the way at a restaurant and pick up something or once he arrived at Holy Rock, he could always get something from the church cafeteria.

Before leaving for Holy Rock, he made a call. "Hey, Pastor. It's Stiles. How are you feeling?"

"Blessed, son. How are you?"

"I'm good, Pastor. I was calling to let you know I'm in Memphis for a couple of weeks, maybe even a little longer. I don't know if you heard, but Pastor Khalil's brother was involved in a serious car crash last week. He needed me to come and take his place so he would be free to be at his brother's side and to support Fancy."

"No, I hadn't heard about that, but it's good to hear you're home, son."

Stiles could hear in his father's voice and tell from his conversation that today was a good day for Pastor. He didn't sound confused in the least bit.

"I'm heading to Holy Rock in a few minutes, but I'll stop by to see you and Josie later today."

"Okay, son. I'll tell Josie. She'll be glad to hear that."

"Is she at home?"

"Yes, she's in the kitchen making us some lunch before our show comes on."

Stiles chuckled. "Okay, Pastor. I love you. I'll see you soon."

"Now who did you say this is?" Pastor asked.

Stiles heart dropped. It was if the wind had been abruptly sucked out of him. "It's Stiles, Pastor. Your son."

"Oh, Stiles. It's good to hear from you, son."

"It's good to hear your voice, Pastor. Like I said, I'll stop by later on this afternoon to see you. Okay?"

"Sure, I'll be looking forward to it."

"Goodbye, Pastor." Stiles ended the call, walked into the hallway, retrieved his car keys and door keys off the key holder, and walked out of the side door and into the garage.

His upbeat attitude sunk immediately after talking to Pastor. Times like these, hearing his father go into the memory fog, was hard for him to bear. "God, you're in charge. Give me the mental fortitude to persevere through any trail you set before me."

He got inside his ride, turned on the ignition, pushed the overhead remote, and backed out of the garage and driveway.

Stiles was drawn from sad thoughts of Pastor by the music on the radio. His soul was immediately fed as he savored the soothing, healing words of a song Full of Grace music ministry had sung several times, "God Will Take care of Me," by VaShawn Mitchell.

Xavier struggled to open his eyes. Why was it such a difficult thing to do? All around him he saw the beauty of the skies and the bright rays of light ushering him closer to the voices. He looked around. At first the images appeared blurry and out of focus, but as he continued to look around they began to clear.

"Xavier," Pepper cried, grabbing hold of his hand and squeezing it. She'd been at the hospital for no more than ten minutes, having come as soon as she'd gotten off of work. It had become part of her daily routine. She left work in the afternoon, stopped by a place to pick up a sandwich and sides to take to the hospital with her, and she would stay until late at night, only to do it all over again the next day. On the weekend, she arrived early in the morning and remained by his side until late at night. One thing she had been glad about was Ian had not come to visit since the encounter he had with Fancy McCoy. He couldn't call Xavier on his phone because it had not been recovered since the accident.

Fancy jumped up from the chair and rushed to his bedside, as did Khalil. Khalil had been sitting in the loveseat style leather sofa in front of Xavier's hospital bed.

"Xavier, thank God, you're back," Fancy squealed, and both hands flew up to her mouth. Looking at Khalil, she said, tears flowing like a broken water pipe, "My baby is awake, Khalil. Xavier's back with us." She wiped the tears and leaned down and planted tiny kisses all over her baby boy's face.

When his mother rose upright, Xavier looked from Fancy's face to Pepper's face and then to his brother. He managed to show a slight smile. Opening his mouth, he tried to push the words out. In his mind, he was able to speak freely, but he found it almost impossible to say the words out loud, but he didn't give up.

"Ma."

"Yes, baby. I'm here. God brought you back to us."

He looked at Pepper. His vision still somewhat scattered, he was still able to make out her cheesy smile. His heart seemed to pick up its pace as his excitement accelerated. Where was he? When he tried to move his body it hurt like hell. He looked and saw his leg was wrapped in what he perceived to be a cast. His torso felt like it had been detached from his body. It was weird. The whole scene before him was weird. His throat ached and his hands felt numb.

"Pepper?"

"Yep, it's me," she giggled. "Boy, am I glad to hear your voice and see those beautiful brown eyes." She also wiped tears away.

What was happening? Why were they crying? Next, he saw his brother. Their eyes locked.

Xavier struggled to speak. Grunts came out instead of words, his throat feeling raw like he had a bad case of strep.

"Hey, there, li'l bro." Khalil walked up from the foot of the bed and stood next to his mother, placing him closer to his brother.

"We should call the nurse," Pepper said.

"Yes, you're right," agreed Khalil. "I'll go tell them he's awake."

Khalil rushed out of the room and went to the nurses' station. Within minutes, he returned with a male nurse by his side.

"So, you decided to awake from your beauty sleep, huh?" the nurse joked while approaching Xavier's bed and reading his vital signs. "I'm going to contact Dr. Daniels. He's going to be happy to hear this."

"Thank you," said Fancy, moving aside from Xavier's bedside to allow the nurse to get closer to Xavier.

"How do you feel?" the nurse asked.

Xavier stared aimlessly at the nurse.

"Do you know where you are?"

Xavier remained confused and incoherent, unsure of what the machines were and where he was. He managed to shake his head in slow motion from side to side.

"You're at Regional One Hospital. You were in a bad car crash. Do you remember that?"

Again, Xavier shook his head no. *Did he say I was in a car crash? How? When?*

Pepper remained planted on the other side of his bed, still holding tightly to his swollen hand. Her emotions were all over the place. She was glad she had been there to see Xavier open his eyes and call *her* name. Only God knows what she would have done had it been Ian who he woke up to and not her. That would have been crushing, but no need to think about that now. The odds were in her favor. She was the one he saw when he opened his eyes. She was the one he would remember being there, not Ian. It couldn't get much better than this.

Ian remained worried sick about Xavier. His sister gave him any news she heard but it wasn't the same as seeing Xavier with his own eyes. Eliana told him Xavier hadn't fully woke up, even after the heavy round of medications had been eased up.

"If I was there, if he heard my voice, then I bet he would wake up. But that trick, Pepper, is up there like she's really his lady. Guess she thinks she's *li'l miss* whatever she thinks she is, since she's got in good with his mother."

"Ian, stop getting yourself all worked up. I don't think Pepper is like that. Before his accident, Xavier and her were, well they were acting like they were a couple. You know that, and you and him rarely hung out anymore," Eliana told him while she sat at desk working on an excel report Stiles had asked her for.

Of course, in her work space, Sista Mavis strained to hear what Eliana was saying. She thought she heard Eliana say her brother's name. On a pretense of needing some paperwork, she got up from her desk, walked toward the open space leading into Eliana's oversized workspace, and opened the supply cabinet.

Eliana looked to her left and saw Sista Mavis standing at the open cabinet door. "Look, Ian, we'll talk later," she whispered. "Ears are wide open here. Love you, and please don't let Pepper or Fancy get next to you. Go back to work. We'll talk this evening."

Ian shuffled in his seat at work. "Yea, but you don't understand. You and Khalil are hitting it off while Xavier and me are, well, let's just say there seems to be no Xavier and me."

"It's not like you were in love with him, Ian. You just hate to lose to anything or anyone. Knowing you the way I do, your relationship with Xavier would have been just another one of your conquests, and you would have moved on to your next victim."

"Ouch," replied Ian. "And this coming from my own sister? How cruel is that?"

Eliana laughed. "You know the truth hurts sometimes."

Ian half laughed too, knowing his sister was probably right. He hated to lose at anything. "I'll talk to you later, sis, but call me before then if you hear anything."

"Okay, I will. Bye now."

Eliana ended the call and then watched from her peripheral as Sista Mavis closed the supply cabinet door.

"Did you find what you were looking for, Sista Mavis?"

Sista Mavis, pretending to be caught off guard, looked over her shoulder at Eliana. "Oh, yes, I did. I found exactly what I was looking for," and proceeded to retreat to her desk.

26

When Stiles left Holy Rock, it was well after six p.m. Eliana remained with him.

"Thank you for staying late this evening, Eliana. I don't know what I would have done without your assistance. You're a true gem."

"Thank you, Minister Stiles. I'm glad I could be of help."

"It's a blessing isn't it that Xavier woke up."

"Yes, it sure is. When Kha-, when Pastor Khalil," she corrected herself, "called with the good news, I couldn't help but give God praise."

"Yes, when I talked to him, I did the same. God is good."

"All the time," Eliana added and they exited the doors of Holy Rock.

Stiles, like he promised, headed to Pastor and Josie's house. On the way, he stopped at a bakery and bought a half dozen of vegan chocolate cupcakes and a half dozen of vegan strawberry and kiwi cupcakes. They loved sweets. Since Josie had changed Pastor to mostly a plant-based diet, she had told him it was hard to find vegan desserts.

Next, he stopped at a Kroger's store and purchased a bouquet of flowers for Josie.

Josie was a godsend to his father. Sometimes Stiles believed he didn't express his appreciation for her in the manner she deserved. Josie had stuck by Pastor through some tough times and now she was proving her unconditional love yet again as Pastor faced a new challenge in his health. He wanted to do something to bring a smile to her face.

Stiles pulled up into the driveway of Emerald Estates, got out of his car, and walked along the path leading to the side entrance.

Knock, knock.

Stiles watched the door slowly open. Josie's face lit up when she saw his face.

Opening the door fully, she stepped to the side and allowed Stiles to come into the house. "Stiles, look at you. Aren't you looking good."

Stiles leaned in and kissed Josie on the cheek. "And you look beautiful as always. Here," he passed the bouquet of mixed flowers to her, "these are for you."

A huge smile formed on her face. "Oh my, thank you. They're beautiful," she exclaimed and smelled the flowers. "Ummm, they smell so good. Come on in here."

Stiles walked further into the house while Josie walked back and closed the side door.

"Your father's in the den watching T.D. Jakes. Go on in there. It's just so good to see you. How long will you be here this time?"

"A couple of weeks at the least. It depends on how long Pastor Khalil needs me. I was telling Pastor when we talked earlier Khalil's brother was in a bad car accident. He and Fancy have been spending most of their time at the hospital, which is why I'm here."

"Yes, your father was trying to tell me something, but he wasn't making much sense, you know. But now I understand."

Stiles entered the den with Josie trailing behind. "Hi, Pastor."

Pastor looked up from his television show and smiled. "Well, well, what a surprise." He started to stand up. "It's good to see you, son."

Pastor fully stood and embraced his son. "What are you doing here?"

"Remember," Stiles stopped and decided not to put the pressure of making Pastor feel he had forgotten their earlier conversation. "I flew in this morning. I'm the associate pastor at Holy Rock now, Pastor. I'm here to fill in for Pastor Khalil. His brother was in an accident."

"Oh, yea, I think I remember you saying something about that. So you took the position, huh?"

Stiles fought back the need to break down. It was just tough, real tough to see the look of unknowing on his father's wrinkly brow. "Uh, yes, Pastor, I accepted the position."

"I'm glad to hear that, son. You know that church means everything to me." Pastor shook his head and sat back down. "What's that you got there?"

Stiles looked at the box in his hand. "Oh, yea, I almost forgot. I brought you and Josie some cupcakes. Vegan cupcakes," he turned and whispered to Josie.

"Wow, you're too much," Josie said. "Look, Pastor. He brought me flowers, too."

"Boy, what you trying to do—steal my woman," Pastor chuckled and leaned back in his chair, tapping his knee.

Stiles and Josie joined in on the laugh. It was good to hear Pastor laugh. It took Stiles' mind off the sadness that had tried to creep into his spirit.

"Let me go put these in a vase." Josie disappeared and Stiles passed the box of cupcakes to Pastor.

She reappeared just as Pastor was opening the box.

"Oh, looka here, looka here, Josie. Chocolate and strawberry cupcakes."

Josie walked up and standing in front of Pastor, eyed the cupcakes. "Ummm, they look delicious."

"Thank you, son. Sit down over there," Pastor ordered and Stiles sat on the sofa while Josie sat in the chair next to Pastor.

"Let's see what we're working with," Pastor said, picking up a strawberry cupcake. "Josie, which do you want?"

"You know me, chocolate every time."

Pastor picked up a chocolate cupcake and passed it to her, then pushed the box toward Stiles.

"I'll pass for now. I've got to get something hardy in my belly first."

"Well, you know you came to the right place."

"You know me, Josie. I was secretly hoping you had cooked."

"Hardly a day goes by that I'm not going to fix me and Pastor a full dinner. You know that."

"That's what I was banking on." Stiles laughed.

"I got plenty of turnip greens, some skillet cornbread, and a big pot of spaghetti. I'll fix you some."

"Josie you need to have your own TV cooking show."

"Boy," Josie threw up her hand and blushed, "you're something else." Josie got up after taking a bite of her cupcake. "These are good. And they're fresh, too."

"I'm glad. The lady told me they were freshly baked."

"You stay in here with your father. I'm going to warm this food up. I'll be done in a minute."

"Thank you, Josie."

"Look over there in the corner," Pastor pointed to the corner in front of him by the television, "and get one of those trays."

Stiles got up and got the tray and brought it back to sit it in front of him.

Josie returned with a plate of food, sat it on the tray and then left out of the den again. She returned with a big glass of sweet iced tea and lemon.

"You know how to spoil me," Stiles said. "Thank you, Josie."

"You're welcome."

Stiles bowed his head and prayed over his food. When he was done, he picked up his fork and began attacking the food.

While he ate, they talked and laughed. Stiles told Pastor for what had to the third time about his new position at Holy Rock and the reason he was in Memphis. They watched one of Pastor and Josie's other favorite TV shows, "Master Chef Junior."

After the program ended, Stiles stretched. "I guess I better get to the other side of town. It's getting late for me and I have another long day tomorrow. I'm going to deliver the message at midweek service. I sure would like it if you two could come."

"I don't think we'll be able to make it. Me and Josie don't get out at night anymore. We don't see as good as we used to and Josie likes to lock up the house before dark. So much is going on out there."

Josie nodded in agreement.

"I can send someone to pick you up, if you'd like and bring you back home."

"No, we don't want you to go through all of that. But if God says the same we'll be there Sunday," Josie said.

"It won't be a problem. I'm sure of it. I wasn't talking about the church van. I'm saying I can get Brother Ron to come and pick you up."

"No, son, we appreciate it, but what Josie says goes." Pastor laughed.

"Okay, if you say so. But I can get him to come and get you Sunday so you don't have to drive."

Stiles could see the look of relief appear on Josie's countenance. She had confided in Stiles before about Pastor sometimes forgetting how to get around in the city, and even his lack of remembering familiar places he once could drive to with his eyes closed, like Holy Rock.

"That would be nice," said Josie as the three of them left out of the den and headed to the kitchen.

"Take this." Josie had made Stiles a to-go plate. "This is in case you get hungry tonight. I put you one chocolate and one strawberry cupcake in the other container."

"But those were for you and Pastor."

"Yes, I know, but we have plenty. Now, here take this food."

Stiles kissed and hugged Josie. "Thank you, Josie. I love you."

"I love you more," Josie replied.

Stiles turned to his father, standing next to Josie and gave him a hug too. "I love you, Pastor. I'll see you guys Sunday."

"Love you, too, son."

"I'll see you Sunday," Stiles said again, then opened the door and stepped outside to be welcomed by the warm night breeze."

He walked toward his car, briefly stopping to look back to make sure Josie closed the door behind him.

27

"The thrill of coming home has never changed."
Guy Pearce

The month of September was just days away. Plans had been made and set for Stiles' installation the second Sunday. Guest preachers, choirs, and churches were invited to attend. The celebration was going to be large with a huge banquet dinner to take place at the Peabody Hotel the night before the installation. It was almost like a replay of the Jubilee Tragedy, but hopefully this would have a far different, and better, outcome.

Xavier was up and moving around, but he was still having trouble with his memory. Dr. Daniels explained to Xavier and his family since he had suffered some brain damage he might experience memory loss and become easily agitated. He still didn't remember being involved in the crash.

Ian had given up on rekindling a relationship with Xavier. The last straw for Ian was when Xavier claimed he was not gay and never had been. He acted like he barely knew who Ian was. This was quite upsetting for Ian. He finally said enough is enough, there were too many other fish in the sea, and it was time for him to let this one bite the dust. Ian didn't know if Xavier was using his accident to avoid his truth, but Ian was fed up with trying to convince him otherwise.

They both had been quite lucky when it came to Leo Jones' murder. The suspect who had been initially arrested did not say or mention seeing Xavier and Ian, which is exactly what Ian tried to convince Xavier of the night he went and wrecked his car and almost killed himself. The man was charged and he also pleaded guilty to committing the murder. News media said the man stated Leo Jones had sexually assaulted him before and the night he murdered him, Leo was trying to sexually assault him again in the alley beside the establishment where Leo's body was found. The man stated that Leo first assaulted him when he first met Leo at the same bar and went with him to a hotel room. He said Leo became violent when he refused certain sexual advancements. When the man told him he wanted to leave, Leo refused to let him leave and then beat him up and sexually assaulted him. He pleaded guilty to second degree murder and was sentenced to seventeen years in prison.

When Ian told Xavier about the case, Xavier became angry and told Ian never to mention anything about Leo Jones to him again. He insisted on Ian leaving his apartment. That was it for Ian. He was so angry that he almost made the decision to tell Pepper all about Leo Jones but decided Xavier wasn't worth the fight. He remembered what Eliana told him months ago when Xavier was still in the hospital--*It's not like you were in love with him, Ian. You just hate to lose to anything or anyone.*

Ian had moved on. He'd never been lacking when it came to finding someone to spend time with. Truth be told, Ian arrived at the conclusion

Xavier was bad news. Xavier was still experiencing difficulty physically and mentally from the accident and Ian was not about to play nursemaid to anyone. He had too much life he wanted to live. He was looking forward to attending the banquet for Stiles Graham with his new found beau. Let's see how that would rock Xavier's boat.

"I'm telling you, Victoria, Stiles is a good man and you're a good woman. I don't see why you think it would be a mistake for me to play matchmaker for the two of you."

"Fancy, it wouldn't work. You know me. I like to *do* things. I mean, I'm adventurous, spontaneous, I'm not the kind of woman who wants to be in church twenty-four seven. You thrive on being at Holy Rock, it's your life, and me, well, I have to literally pry myself out of the bed on Sunday mornings."

"Uh, you're acting like I'm saying you're going to marry the man." Fancy nudged her best friend and laughed.

"She's right, Victoria. What would it hurt to meet the man?" Tara interjected. The three ladies were gathered at Victoria's house, getting ready to go to a play at the Orpheum Theatre.

"Doing things like what we're doing now is what I like. His idea of fun is probably going to Bible study every week."

"You are so crazy," Tara said.

"Which is why I think you should meet him," Fancy pressed. "He needs someone to make him laugh again, someone who will bring him out of that self-imposed shell he has himself in. The man has been hurt so much that I think he's terrified to trust his feelings. He's closed himself off to having a real relationship again, to having fun. You're just the woman who can open him up."

Victoria looked at Fancy. This time she didn't laugh or counter with a smart rebuttal. "You're serious about this, aren't you?"

"You darn right I am. So, here's what we're going to do. I'm going to introduce the two of you at the banquet Saturday night. You'll sit at my table."

"Hold up, up front? At *your* table?"

"Yep, at my table."

"But isn't that going to be at the head table? I do not want to be sitting at the head table. I'll feel like I'm in a zoo or something. Everybody watching you eat and whatever."

"There is no *head* table. Stiles didn't want that. Our table will be in the center of the room. It's going to be me, Xavier, and I'm sure he's going to bring Pepper."

Victoria smiled at hearing her daughter would be accompanying Xavier. Since meeting Xavier, Pepper was like a different girl. She was at church just about every Sunday, something that Victoria used to have to force her to do when she was a teen. She didn't run around clubbing or hanging out. Most of her time was spent with Xavier, and Xavier despite the gay rumors that had circulated about the young man, seemed to be into Pepper as well, so Victoria no longer entertained those thoughts.

"Who else is going to be at the table?"

"Khalil, of course, and whoever his guest will be, you, Stiles, Stiles' parents and Cynthia Jones, Leo Jones' widow."

"What about you, Tara?"

"Girl, I will be with my boo and kids. We already have our table reserved, so do what the lady wants. This is your time, your turn to have a good man in your life. It's not all about Stiles Graham."

"Tara's right. You deserve someone to love you and treat you with respect and kindness."

"Uh, we may not even like each other."

"Okay, if you don't hit it off there's nothing lost, but what if you find out you can't keep your hands off each other. Would that be so bad?"

"Well, he *is* a fine piece of chocolate." Victoria giggled.

"You got that right," Tara agreed.

"He *is* that," said Fancy, remembering the kiss they'd shared, but then quickly dismissing it out of her mind.

"Okay, I'm in."

"Whoohooo, it's on," screamed Fancy and kicked up her legs.

"This is going to be so much fun," Tara said and the three ladies got up from their seats.

"Now, let's get out of here before we miss all the good parking spaces. You know how parking is downtown. And this play is sold out, so the earlier we get there the better."

"I'm behind you," Fancy said.

"Let's go," said Victoria as thoughts about the possibility of being in a relationship with a preacher and pastor filtered through her mind. A bit of nervousness caused her tummy to rumble, but she quickly dismissed it and replaced it with some *what if it does work* thoughts.

28

"Somewhere between heartaches and waiting comes another chance to be found by someone who can show you that you are not just an option but the only choice." Unknown

The banquet was first class. From the music to the food to the ambiance. It was like a fine dining restaurant mixed with an upscale nightclub type of atmosphere.

Khalil had made it clear when the banquet was being planned that he wanted a live DJ and a wide array of divine tasting food. There was a space set up for a dance floor. Several couples danced to Pop songs and R&B tunes, with all of the music being tastefully chosen for such an event. It was good, clean fun.

Khalil despised when churches had stuck up, run of the mill, boring functions. He was a young man who still liked his secular music and having a good time. He wanted his congregation to feel comfortable even when attending an event such as this. For instance, after their annual New Years' Eve watch service, they brought in the new year with a big New Year's Eve bash held in the youth center at Holy Rock, complete with the same things as tonight's event, just more. There was good food, good fun, dancing, laughing, a time to celebrate.

Fancy introduced Stiles and Victoria. She had already told Khalil and Xavier her plans to play matchmaker. They didn't like the idea of their mother interfering in the lives of others and their relationships, but they put up little protest.

Xavier thought Victoria was a cool lady. Pepper had a lot of her ways. As for Khalil, as long as it detracted Stiles and his mother from each other, he was good with it. He didn't know much about Victoria Rawlings, but he surmised if his mother was cool with her then he had no qualms about her.

Khalil leaned in and whispered to Eliana, "You look beautiful."

Eliana looked at him and whispered back, "Thank you." She was glad she listened to her best friend, Carol. Buying and then having the nerve to wear the chic red maxi, off the shoulder, mermaid style dress with flare sleeves was out of her comfort zone. But it seemed to pay off after Khalil told her for the third time how beautiful she looked.

Xavier and Pepper engaged in light conversation as Pepper sneaked every opportunity to people watch, really looking for Ian. Xavier had come a long way since his car crash but for now he still relied on a wheelchair for mobility. There were times he sunk into a depressed state whenever he thought about what could have happened and why he intentionally did what he did. He hadn't confessed to anyone that his desire at the time was to kill himself. Though those suicidal thoughts had passed, they were replaced with guilt and self-condemnation for doing something so stupid as to crash his car. He'd already been stuck in a wheelchair for almost a month. He understood how his father must have felt not being able to move about like he once did. Thank God he had great family support.

Pepper was another source of support for Xavier. She had been by his side since day one, from what his mother told him. Every day after she got off work she headed for his house. They practically lived together because most nights, she didn't go home. She took care of his needs. His mother and home health aides tended to him during the day and a CNA remained on call for his weekend care. "Do you want to dance?"

Xavier shook his head. "Really?" He found himself growing agitated at Pepper. "What kind of stupid question is that?"

"Uh, who says you have to be on your feet to dance, Xavier? Look out there. Do any of the people on that dance floor look like they're from "So You Think You Can Dance?" All you have to do is move your body. Think of it as a form of exercise.

"Nah, I don't think so.

"Xavier, all you have to do is move your arms and body to the beat of the music from your wheelchair." She giggled.

Xavier didn't find it funny. "I don't think so."

"Aww, come on. I'll push you onto the dance—"

"I said *no*. Now back off will ya," Xavier yelled. Those sitting at the table stopped their conversations and eating to look at the couple.

"What's going on?" Victoria asked.

"Nothing, Mom."

"Xavier, what's going on?" Fancy asked.

"Didn't you hear Pepper? It's nothing. Look, I'm tired. I'm ready to go home."

"But, Xavier, you haven't been here a good hour, and they haven't served dinner yet."

"I'm not hungry. I want to go home. Now."

Pepper stood up. "I'll take him. No worries."

"No, I'll take him," Fancy insisted.

"Really, I don't mind. We came here together so I'll take him home. Anyway, I'm a little tired myself. Plus, you're needed here more than me and Xavier. Don't you agree, Xavier?"

"Yea, Ma. I'm sorry. I don't mean to ruin your evening."

Khalil and Stiles reappeared at the table almost simultaneously after having worked the room to meet and greet people in attendance.

"What's going on?" Khalil asked. "Ruin her evening how?"

Fancy threw up a hand, "Oh, it's nothing. Xavier is worn out. He's ready to go home. I told him I would take him but Pepper insists."

"You all right, bruh?"

"Yea, just not into this right now. I thought I would be but all the people and folks constantly coming up wanting to talk and all....I'm not feeling it. You know?"

Khalil nodded. "Yea, I feel ya." Khalil looked at Pepper. "You sure you got this? I can always take him home and come back."

"No, I'm good. You ready, Xavier?" She looked down at him.

"Yea."

"Wait, let us at least fix you something to eat to take with you."

"Sure," Pepper said. "You okay with that, Xavier?"

"Yea, that's straight."

"Stay here, Ma. I'll go tell the caterers."

Stiles returned to his chair. "Xavier, you sure you're all right, man?"

"Yes, I'm good," he said, barely audible.

Stiles' eyes veered over to Victoria. Her smile lit up her face. Stiles swallowed deeply when he saw her stroll across the floor and back to the table after talking to some of the guests. He was definitely attracted to her. She was quite an attractive woman. Her honey complexion glowed. She wore just the right amount of makeup, and her natural hair was flawless.

Victoria and Fancy had gone shopping earlier in the week and Victoria chose an elegant, form-fitting, tan with black accents midi-dress that sported a V-neck with cape sleeves.

Khalil returned to the table rather quickly. "They're preparing your food. You can head toward the exit and they're going to meet you there. You should see them when they come out of the side door in the hallway. There should be plenty of everything."

"Thanks, bruh. Nite, Ma. Good seeing everyone," Xavier said.

Those at the table replied with "Good night, feel better," and so on.

Fancy stood up, went over to her son and kissed him on the side of his forehead. She did the same to Pepper, and squeezed Pepper's hand. "Thank you, Pepper. You're a godsend."

"I'll talk to you later, sweetheart," Victoria told her daughter. "Be careful out there. Text me when you make it home."

"Okay, I will. Have a good time." She waved goodbye and she and Xavier left for the exit.

Ian was beside himself when Eliana told him he had missed Xavier at the banquet by mere minutes. He had gone out of his way to arrive late, hoping he would stand out among the crowd and Xavier would see him and become jealous. It all backfired. Once again, Pepper had come between them. This was it. Ian mentally threw his hands up in the air. Enough was enough. He could have any man he wanted. That was evident in the arm candy he brought to the banquet. The man was not only handsome, but he was a wealthy, successful banker who came from a long line of money and he didn't mind spending it on Ian. *You know what, Xavier, I gotchu. Watch what I tell you.*

29

"If you carry the bricks from your past relationship, you will end up building the same house." KushandWizdom

Victoria led the conversation with Stiles. They had exchanged pleasantries, but to keep from feeling awkward sitting next to him, she thought she would start a friendly conversation. "So, are you excited to be back in Memphis?"

Stiles looked at her. His mind was thinking lustful thoughts, something he hadn't done in a while, not since he and Kareena's relationship fiasco.

"Yes, I'm grateful God has blessed me to keep my church in Houston while returning to my first love."

"Well, Holy Rock is glad to have you back. The banquet is nice, isn't it?"

"Yes, I can't believe all of this is for me. It makes me feel, well almost a little embarrassed at the attention, you know."

Victoria smiled and Stiles returned her smile with a warm smile of his own, melting a piece of Victoria's heart. *Dang, he is so fine. And those lips. OMG and look at those perfect white teeth.*

"Would you like to dance?" Khalil asked Eliana.

"I'm not a very good dancer," she confessed.

"Neither am I."

"Uh, that's not what I heard," she countered, laughing.

"And what did you hear?"

"That you can give Chris Brown a run for his money."

"Lady, are you serious? I wish. Come on, let me prove it to you."

Without waiting on her response, he stood from the table, reached down and grabbed her hand. Eliana didn't put up a big fuss. She allowed him to lead her to the dance floor, both of them giggling along the way.

From a nearby table, Sista Mavis watched. *I knew it. They can't tell me nothing is going on between them two.*

Ian walked into the banquet with a relatively conservative looking white man. Both of them were dressed in black suits. Ian was a handsome guy and his friend was equally as handsome with a reddish short beard and red hair.

Sista Mavis spotted him as they walked pass the dance floor, temporarily blocking her view of Pastor Khalil and Eliana. *Umm, that's Eliana's brother, I think. That must be his little boy toy. Guess Victoria's little fast tale daughter scared Xavier straight.* She burst out laughing at her own thoughts.

Sista Mavis, what are you laughing about?" one of the ladies sitting at the table with her asked.

"Oh, nothing. Just watching these young folks on the dance floor."

Ian walked past her and she regained her view of Khalil and Eliana, as well as some other couples dancing. She turned back around in her chair to face the people at her table. "When I was growing up in church, there was no way you would be dancing and playing that secular music, and at a church too? I think it's disrespecting the Lord's name."

"Now, Sista Mavis, no need to get yourself upset," one of the deacons sitting at the table told her. "There's nothing we can do about it, so let it go. That's between the Lord and Pastor Khalil."

"I don't see anything wrong with it," the lady sitting to the right of the deacon said. "I'd rather have them having clean fun in the church than to be out in these streets doing God knows what."

"I guess it comes with having a young pastor like Pastor Khalil," another lady to the left of her added.

"Humph, I'm like Sista Mavis, I don't agree with it," the husband of the lady said.

"Wrong is wrong and right is right and this is wrong," said Sista Mavis, and picked up her glass of tea and took a swallow before placing her glass back on the table.

The deacon patted her hand. "It's all right, Sista Mavis. I don't think anyone is going to go to hell because of it."

Sista Mavis rolled her eyes at the man and turned back around.

Pastor Khalil and Eliana were dancing to an upbeat song, laughing and giggling like they were two lovebirds. *She wants to be the First Lady. I guess he does need himself a good woman. If I have to say so myself, Eliana is a sweet girl. She might just make him a good wife.*

God knows he needs one with all those heifers running around the church after that poor man.

Sista Mavis scanned the room. *Yea, look at 'em. Young girls eying him like he a piece of fine chocolate. Some of these old women lusting after that boy, too. They ought to be ashamed.* She shook her head and then returned her focus to her table.

"How are you and the kids?" Stiles asked Cynthia who was seated next to him. The new widow still looked lost. She and Leo attended every church function together. Now, here she sat all alone and hurting. Knowing the man responsible for her husband's death pled guilty and would be behind bars for years, did little to soothe her pain. Her grief was still raw.

"The kids are okay. They miss their daddy. It's hardly a day that passes when they don't ask me when he's coming home. They're still young and they don't understand."

"And you?"

"What *about* me?"

"How are *you* doing, Cynthia?"

"All I can say is I'm coping. Leo and I were soulmates. Living without him has been hard. I mean as far as financially, I don't have any worries. Leo made sure if anything ever happened to him that his family would be well provided for. But it does little to make me feel better. I miss him, Stiles. I miss my husband." Her eyes swelled with tears.

Victoria watched but heard little of the conversation exchanged between Stiles and Cynthia. Everyone at their table was chatting and the sounds of chatter from the other tables made it almost impossible to decipher what was being said.

Stiles' heart was heavy for Cynthia. He caressed her hand that lay on the table. "Let's not talk about it now. I don't want to see you upset. We'll talk later."

She nodded and then looked down in her lap and opened the small purse. Removing a tissue, she kept her head down and swiftly wiped her eyes.

Closing the purse and looking back up at Stiles she said, "Thank you. You were always such a good friend to Leo."

Their conversation was interrupted by servers placing basket of rolls on the tables and refreshing the guests' beverages.

There was a short program recognizing Stiles as the new associate pastor of Holy Rock. Khalil spoke highly of him, followed by words from two of the staff ministers, chairman of the deacon board, Pastor, and lastly Fancy spoke. When they were done, it was Stiles' turn.

He approached the podium set up at the front of the banquet space. "Thank you for all the eloquent words said about me and on my behalf. God is a good God. I tell you, I am one blessed man. God has poured so much of His favor over my life. To be given an opportunity to be part of the church I grew up in, the church founded by my father," he pointed over to his table where Pastor sat, " to have my father here to see me return to Holy Rock, and to have Holy Rock welcome me back, is one of the greatest joys of my life. To Pastor McCoy," he looked at Khalil and he saw the young woman next to Khalil with a smile on her face, "thank you for asking me to be the associate pastor. I will serve with honor. I will be by your side whenever you need me. I must say it is remarkable to see how you are growing in the ministry. To be a man as young as you with the wisdom you have is a God thing. Since you've been the shepherd of this great church, Holy Rock has blossomed into an international ministry."

The audience applauded and stood up to give Khalil a standing ovation. Stiles joined in and applauded as well.

Fancy was proud of her son. This was a night set aside for Stiles but Stiles had taken the spotlight off of himself and placed it on Khalil. She was overwhelmed with joy.

When the audience settled down and began taking their seats, Stiles continued. "You're going to go even farther, young man. Keep being obedient to what God tells you to do. Keep allowing him to lead you and direct your path. He will show you favor like none other. I'm a living witness He will."

Stiles said a few more words before taking his seat. The remainder of the banquet people continued to eat, mingle, dance, and have fun.

Toward the end of the evening, Stiles and Victoria talked some more. Not very much because neither of them wanted to disregard the others at the table. Stiles paid attention to his father, Josie, and to Cynthia. Victoria understood and actually she was pleased to see how attentive he was toward them. Just like Fancy said, Stiles Graham appeared to be a good and honorable man.

"Well, I think I'm going to leave. If I plan to attend all three services tomorrow, I better get home and get some rest," she said to Stiles.

"I'll be right behind you. I have to take my parents home and Sista Cynthia. Then I'm going to do the same. You know, it was nice having you sitting next to me, Sister Victoria."

Victoria smiled. She hoped she hadn't turned two shades of red because she felt all giddy. "The feeling is mutual."

"Let me walk you to your car."

"Oh, thank you."

Fancy watched and listened. *Yessss!*

Stiles pushed his chair back and stood up from the table. "Pastor, Josie, Cynthia, I'll be right back. I'm going to walk this lovely lady to her car. We'll be ready to leave when I get back, if that's okay with you all."

"It's fine with me. I need to get home so the sitter can get home. I told her I wouldn't be out late," explained Cynthia.

"Sure," said Stiles.

"We're ready whenever you are," said Josie. "Right, Pastor?"

"Huh? What? What's going on?"

"Nothing, sweetheart," Josie said, shaking her head, smiling and kissing her hubby on the cheek.

Fall was approaching and the weather outside was perfect. Stars lined the skies and the moon shown bright.

"It's a beautiful night."

"Yes, it is," Stiles agreed as they walked toward the parking lot.

"My car is right over there." Victoria pointed to her white Altima.

"Oh, okay. So, Sister Victoria, tell me, how long have you been a member of Holy Rock? I don't remember seeing you when I was pastor or even before then. I'm sure I would have remembered you," he flirted. *Did I just say that?*

"I've been a member for a number of years. I hate to admit it, but I didn't come that often. My name was on the church roll but that's about it. It's only been the last year that I made a commitment to give God more of my time."

"I understand, and believe me I don't judge. That's for God. The important thing is to have a relationship with God. It doesn't mean you have to take a space on the church pew every Sunday. Although as a pastor I encourage my members to attend church as often as possible. I liken it to a person taking multi-vitamins. They're good for you and you can rarely overdose on vitamins."

Stiles and Victoria laughed and continued walking slowly toward her car. "I'm not trying to get all preachy on you," he apologized.

"No, I didn't take it like that. I mean, you're a man of God. I wouldn't expect anything less."

They arrived at her car. "Yes, I *am* a man of God but I'm also a man. I don't like to shove my faith and beliefs down anyone's throat."

"You haven't and you didn't."

Pause.

Nervous, Victoria looked away and opened her handbag and retrieved her car keys. She hit the FOB, remote started the car, and unlocked the door.

Stiles reached in front of her. She could smell his minty breath intermingled with his fragrant cologne. An unexpected but welcomed heat filled the space between them.

"Let me get that." He opened the door for her. *She smells so gooood. Ahhhh.*

"Thanks for walking me to my car."

"No problem. I wanted to make sure you were safe. I'm sure they have security around here somewhere, but my parents taught me to be a gentleman."

There goes that smile again. Well, I'm sure grateful for your parents. *Did that sound corny? Ughh. Come on, Victoria. You can do better than that.*

"I am too." *What's going on with me? I sound so lame. Should I ask for her phone number? What if she turns me down? Why would I ask anyway when I don't want to be involved with anyone? Who says I would be getting involved with her? But I do need to make friends since I'll be coming back and forth to Memphis. I can't expect Fancy to drop everything when I come, and I sure can't expect it of Cynthia. The woman has small kids and she's trying to piece her life back together without Leo. I mean, there're some guys I know I can hang out with. But, I'm not trying to get my heart run over anymore, but I do have needs. That's just the truth. Stop overthinking, dummy.*

"Drive safe, Sister Victoria."

"Okay, thank you, and gnite, Reverend Graham."

"If you insist on calling me Reverend Graham, then how can I ask for your phone number?" *Smile.*

"And if you insist on calling me Sister Victoria how can I expect you to—Stiles?" Victoria flashed a smile of her own, grateful her parents had made her get corrective braces as a teen.

"All right now, Victoria. May I have your phone number? Maybe when I'm in Memphis we can have lunch or dinner sometimes. No pressure, of course."

"No pressure and I'd like that, Stiles."

30

*"There is something beautiful about all scars of
whatever nature. A scar means the hurt is over,
the wound is closed and healed, done with."*
Harry Crews

Ian and his new friend got ready for church.
Ian hadn't walked through the doors of Holy
Rock since Xavier's accident. He had no desire to
and he was only attending today because he
hoped Xavier would be there. If Xavier wasn't
there or if he didn't give him the time of day then
Ian was certain he was going to be done with
trying to prove himself.

Xavier decided he was not going to return to
Holy Rock until he was on his feet again. He
hated being confined to a wheelchair and unable
to get around like he was used to doing. Every
time he transferred to that dumb wheelchair, it
reminded him of what he'd done. He was sick of
beating up on himself. The only way he believed
he could move forward with his life was to be
completely healthy and whole again. Until that
day came, he would stay inside, away from the
public eye. Enough of the coddling that he got
from well-meaning people at Holy Rock. Plus, he
didn't want to run into Ian. He thought of him
often, and part of him missed him terribly, but
the other part of him blamed Ian for the bad

decisions he'd made, starting with the night he let Ian talk him into going to the club.

Initially, after the accident, he didn't remember much of what happened, but as time lapsed, his memory began to return.

No, he hadn't gone inside the club, but still look what had happened—he saw Leo, had to listen to his taunts again, and the end result was Leo got himself *murdered. Good for him. Forgive me, God but it's how I feel.*

"You should go, Pepper. You've been here all weekend. I know you're sick of being stuck in this apartment with me. So go on to church."

"I am not going to leave you by yourself, Xavier."

"I'll be okay. I know how to transfer into my chair if I want something to eat, or if I have to go to the bathroom. Why do you think they kept me in rehab for a month after I was released from the hospital? It was to teach me how to maneuver with this cast. So, please, go. Tell my mother I'm okay so she won't be worried."

Pepper thought for a minute before making her decision. "Okay, but I'm going to the first service and then I'm coming back."

"But the installation services aren't taking place until the third service."

"I don't care; I'm not interested in some installation service. They're boring."

"Okay, suit yourself. Just as long as you go. Do you have something to wear?"

"Sure. I washed the clothes I left over here this past week. I'll put on a pair of jeans and a pullover."

"Okay, cool."

Pepper left out of the bedroom and went into the bathroom and showered. The warm water relaxed her. She pined for the time Xavier would be back on his feet and able to join her. Hopefully, on his next visit Dr. Daniels would remove the cast and give him the okay to start getting up on his leg.

So far, the brain damage Dr. Daniels told him about hadn't really seemed to affect Xavier. Yes, he sometimes got moody and it was easier for him to get angry, but it wasn't too far out of the ordinary that it caused her to be overly concerned.

She came out of the bathroom in Pepper fashion. Xavier looked at her with wanting. It usually took her physically touching him for his body to become aroused. This morning was different. He found himself becoming excited without prompts.

Pepper walked over and sat on the bed while reaching behind her to grab her jeans from the other side of the bed.

Xavier sat fully up in the bed, and as she turned and leaned to get the jeans, he grabbed hold of her until they were face to face.

Pepper looked at him curiously. "What's up?" Unsure what was going on inside that mind of his.

"This..." he pulled back the bed covers.

Pepper smiled and without exchanging more words, Xavier pulled her 110-lb frame easily and covered any space that may have been between them. Their mouths united and their tongues explored each other's like they were in search for sunken treasure. His hands made music with her softness and his excitement coursed through her crevice.

Barely able to talk, the eagerness she felt from him gave her a new sense of urgency, but she spoke anyway. "Guess I'll be missing the first service." His deep kisses kept her from saying another word. All that escaped from her throat were whimpers of pleasure in tune with his guttural moans.

31

"I can't change the direction of the wind, but I can adjust my sails to always reach my destination."
Jimmy Dean

*S*tiles' installation service filled Pastor's heart with joy. The service opened with music by Holy Rock's choir following two songs by the guest choir, one which was Full of Grace. He felt proud that his church had turned out strong. Kareena, River, and some of the deacons were seated close to the front of the church and could easily be seen by Stiles. Other members were lined up on the pews behind them. Just about every member, if not every member, of the choir was present and accounted for. They sung his favorite song," God Will Take Care of Me."

An installation service for an associate pastor wasn't the norm, but in Khalil McCoy fashion, Khalil didn't care about the norm. He wanted to recognize Stiles in this manner and he was glad he did. He read the scripture reading and one of two guest pastors rendered the invocation

Normally, at a regular installation service, there would be a guest sermon but Stiles was given this charge. "It's a blessing and certainly a privilege to stand before you this afternoon in the capacity of associate pastor of this divine church, Holy Rock Ministries. I want to first acknowledge God, then Pastor Khalil McCoy for extending this invitation to me. I thank him for giving me a second chance to come back to Memphis in this honorable position of associate pastor. I want to thank my Houston family, Full of Grace Ministries, for traveling to Memphis to share in this special occasion. Will you all please stand." He extended his hand out toward the congregation. Over 200 people stood to their feet. The remaining congregation clapped. "And the choir," he turned and extended his hand again for Full of Grace Ministries choir. "Thank you Full of Grace choir. For those of you who may not know, that song they just sang by VaShawn Mitchell is one of my favorites. How many of you are a witness that God will take care of you?"

Another round of applause, Amens, and Hallelujahs resonated through the expansive sanctuary.

"I think it's appropriate that I take my text from Matthew chapter eighteen, verse twenty-one, English Standard Version: Then Peter came up and said to him, 'Lord, how often will my brother sin against me, and I forgive him? As many as seven times?' Jesus said to him, 'I do not say to you seven times, but seventy-seven times.' Today, allow me for just a short time to talk about "Second Chances."

His twenty minute sermon stirred the over capacity crowd and people could be heard shouting and praising God as he delivered the Word.

The last part of the service, Khalil returned to the pulpit and gave Stiles his duties.

Stiles, in response, promised to uphold the duties of associate pastor.

"There will be a reception in the church banquet hall for our associate pastor, Full of Grace members, as well as our visiting pastors and choirs. We want to feed you before you leave our presence," Khalil announced after the benediction.

Fancy mingled with the guests and met many of the members from Full of Grace, including Kareena, whom she found to be a beautiful, graceful woman. It was a shame Stiles let her slip through his fingers, but then again, as Fancy thought about it, it was a good thing because from what Victoria said, last night was a success. Stiles had asked Victoria for her phone number, and Victoria said he even called, not texted, her last night to make sure she made it home safely, and to ask her if she would be attending his installation services today. Fancy was ecstatic. Maybe Victoria and Stiles' would find love and happiness in each other, and she would be responsible for it!

She took a brief exit out of the banquet hall to check on Xavier. She hadn't seen or heard from him or Pepper. She ran into Victoria as she was getting ready to enter the banquet hall.

"Hey, girl, you look good."

"Thanks, Fancy. I like that suit you're wearing too. Girl, can you believe I'm here? You know me, normally by this time of afternoon I'm at home chillin' and watching The Real Housewives or something or getting ready for work tomorrow."

"I told you the two of you were going to hit it off." Fancy laughed.

"I don't know. It's too early to tell. But anyway, I like him. So get to praying for a sista."

"I already am. Look, have you heard from Pepper? I didn't see Xavier or her at the first or second service and I still haven't seen them."

"Yes, Pepper texted me and told me she planned on coming to first service but Xavier wanted to stay in."

"Oh, I better call and check on him. I hope he's all right. I still worry about him."

"I don't think anything's wrong. I believe they were just tired from last night."

"Okay, but I'm going to make a quick call just to make sure."

"Girl, you worry too much. Anyway, I'm going in here and see if I can speak to Reverend Graham and then I'm going to get out of here."

"Okay, I'll talk to you this week. Keep me posted if you hear from him."

"You know I will." With that, Victoria vanished into the banquet hall.

"Honey, are you okay?" Fancy asked when Xavier answered the phone. "I didn't see you at church."

"I changed my mind. I wasn't feeling it today."

"Are you sure nothing's wrong?" Fancy pressed.

"Ma, didn't I say I was good? Now, please stop treating me like a kid."

"I'm sorry, son. I just worry about you. That's all."

"No need. Like I said, I'm good."

Fancy heard the aggravation in the tone of his voice. He used to be such a mild-mannered young man, easy going, and slow to anger, but now he could snap at a moment's notice. She told herself it was the effects of the brain injury. *Do not take it personally, Fancy.*

"Okay, well, I'll bring you something to eat when I leave church. The installation service has ended and I'm at the reception now."

"Don't do that. Pepper already got us something. Plus, we still have food left from last night. They packed a lot."

"Oh, good. Well, I'm going to go back into this reception. I'll check on you later."

"Yea, bye, Ma." The call ended before she could respond. She shook her head and then turned to go back into the hall but stopped when she heard someone say, "Excuse me?"

Fancy looked around and met the most gorgeous eyes belonging to none other than Dr. Daniels.

"Aren't you, uh, my patient's mother? Xavier McCoy?"

Fancy smiled. "Yes, I am, Dr. Daniels. What are you doing here?"

"My pastor is the one who gave the first invocation. I'm his head deacon. I accompany him when he visits other churches as much as I can, or when time permits. And you?"

"My son is the senior pastor. Khalil McCoy."

"Oh, I recall you saying your son was a pastor but I didn't put two and two together—you know Xavier McCoy and Khalil McCoy."

"That's understandable. It's a small world, isn't it, Dr. Daniels?"

"Yes, it is. And please, call me Micah." He extended his hand toward Fancy.

"And you should call me Fancy," she said coyly.

"Fancy? What an interesting name. I like it. It suits you perfectly."

"Thank you. Uh, were you going to the reception?"

"Yes, I am. And you?"

"Yes, I just stepped out here for a minute to check on my son."

"Xavier?"

"Yes."

"What? Is he experiencing complications?"

"Oh, nothing like that. It's just me being a mother, you know."

Micah smiled and Fancy thought her heart would melt.

"Did your wife come with you?"

"No. I don't have a wife. Is your husband...or boyfriend here with you?"

"No, I don't have a husband...or a boyfriend."

"Umm, looks like we have something in common already, Fancy. Shall we go inside?"

"Yes, we shall." she blushed again and they walked into the banquet hall.

32

*"You meet thousands of people and none of them
really touch you. And then you meet one person
and your life is changed forever."*
Love & Other Drugs

"Your installation ceremony was nice."

"Yea, it was. I was glad to look out in the congregation and see you sitting there. You were almost front and center."

"Can you believe it? I usually sit as close to the back exit as possible."

"Oh, I see. You're one of those people who like to dash out before the benediction."

"Yea, you got me."

Stiles and Victoria chuckled. He was at home relaxing in his man cave and Victoria was at home in her lady lair, drinking a glass of Moscato. She often closed her evening with a glass of wine. It helped her mentally relax and get her in the frame of mind for the next day.

Stiles was drawn to Victoria like a bee to pollen. In the 24 hours he'd officially known her, she had made him laugh more than he'd laughed in a long time. He learned, unlike Kareena who was just twenty something years old, Victoria was thirty-nine, closer to his 44 years. It wasn't that their ages made a difference, but it still felt nice to have someone closer in age.

"How much longer will you be in Memphis?"

"I'll be flying back to Houston Saturday morning."

"Oh, so you'll be here for the rest of the week."

"Yes, and I won't return until November, unless I'm needed or wanted in Memphis before that time."

Pause.

"Is that right?"

"Yes, you never know when Pastor Khalil might have a change of plans and needs me to fill in for him."

They continued to laugh and talk for almost an hour.

"Well, I guess I better let you go. You have work tomorrow and so do I."

"I enjoyed talking to you, Stiles."

"Same here. Hey, if you have time or if you want to, I'd like to take you to dinner before I leave."

"Dinner?"

"Yes. I mean, if you're interested. I thought since we didn't get a chance to really talk this weekend, maybe we could spend some time getting to know each other. I could use a friend in Memphis."

"What about Fancy and the other ministers and their wives?"

"You're right, but there's something about you that makes me want us to become better acquainted." Stiles hoped he wasn't being too forward or worse yet acting like a wuss. He wanted to get to know Victoria but he didn't want to give her the impression he was looking for anything serious. He wanted what he told her he wanted, a friend. That's it, nothing more. If she wasn't down with that then he had her pegged all wrong from the jump.

"Dinner would be good. You can call or shoot me a text and let me know when." She tried to stifle her yawn. The wine was doing what it was intended to do, make her relax.

"Okay, that's my signal. You get some rest, Victoria."

"I'm sorry, I didn't mean to yawn in the phone."

"No, it's no problem. Have a good night and we'll talk tomorrow."

"Okay, goodnight, Stiles."

"Gnite."

Khalil lay in his bed, hands propped behind his head, thinking about the success of this weekend's events. Everything had gone off without a hitch, and even better than he expected. Stiles had been received with open arms back into the family of Holy Rock. That would give Khalil more freedom to pursue some other things he had planned to expand his ministry and his pockets. So far, he wasn't doing so bad. As a matter of fact, he was doing darn good, better than good.

He looked around his room, surveying his blessings. Music streamed in the background from his playlist. His mind shifted to something his mother had said. *It's time for you to find your first lady.* Could she be right? Did he need to settle down? Could he settle down? Since he and Eliana had been messing around, he had tamed his wild hair somewhat and dismissed a lot of the females he once allowed into his circle. None of them were wifey material. If he put any real thought into it, he would have to say Eliana was the only one who met the criteria of being his ideal First Lady. They had little tension, and she seemed to get him. She wasn't the jealous type even after seeing how some of the ladies at Holy Rock flaunted themselves around him. Eliana let it roll off her like water rolled off oil. She was one of the type of people who could cuss you out without using a cuss word and without you knowing she had 'cussed' you out. Khalil laughed at the thought.

Looking to the left of him, he picked up the remote and turned off the music and flicked on the television to see if there was a game on or a movie perhaps that was watchable on Netflix. He would push thoughts about finding a first lady out of his mind—for now.

Fancy curled up on her sofa with a sandwich and a glass of iced tea. *Maybe I need to get myself a dog or a cat.* She laughed out loud. *Me with a pet running around the house? Nah, on second thought, nix that.*

She thought maybe having a dog or cat around the house would help erase the loneliness that sometimes washed over her when she was all alone at home. She had been used to having Hezekiah around, even though he spent hours upon hours away at Holy Rock, or God knows whatever he would be out there doing. But she found peace in knowing he would be home sooner or later. Then there were the boys. They always had something going on, something to keep her busy. Now that she wasn't spending as much time at Holy Rock, hardly any time at Holy Rock, to be honest, she found it more difficult to fill up her days. But the nights were the worse.

As much as she didn't want to think about either one of them, she thought about Hezekiah and Winston. How could she have wasted so many years being duped by Hezekiah? Back in the day no one could tell her anything about her husband. He was attentive to her needs and thought nothing of lavishing her with gifts from diamonds to pearls, to jet setting vacations, the finest of designer purses and clothes. Anything she wanted, Hezekiah would give it. One thing he didn't give though was access to their money. What had she been thinking to let the man put everything in his name? I mean what sane woman or person does that? Was she that blindly in love with him? It was apparent she was. How else could she account for her stupidity and foolishness?

Then there was Mr. Winston *aka sleaze ball* Washington. Tall, good-looking, successful, kind, a pretty good lay, and someone who didn't mind showering her with his time and attention. In the end, he was nothing but a poisonous snake spewing his vicious lies and deceit into her life. He had played on her to the point she understood why Stiles guarded his heart and his love. It made perfect sense to her now.

Running into Dr. Daniels at Holy Rock was a welcomed distraction. He was the last person she would ever expect to see at her church, yet there he was. To top it off, he recognized her. Of all the number of patients and people she was sure he saw on a daily basis, he remembered her. When he asked for her number she told herself not to expect him to call, and if he did, she was not going to lose her cool. It would be good to have a male companion. Someone who she could laugh and talk to, maybe hang out with from time to time, but nothing serious. Her trust levels were at an all-time low and her radar at an all-time high. He would be just a friend—nothing more. It was her time to be on top, to speak her truth and to do her. No more falling head over heels for any man, no matter how good he appeared. *Fool me once, shame on you, fool me twice, shame on me.*

33

"It has been a long time. I am so glad to be coming back home." Wang Zhizhi

Benny arrived and parked outside of the federal penitentiary in Millington, Tennessee waiting and watching. After sitting in the parking lot scrolling through his phone for the past hour and a half, he looked up and saw the familiar figure walking out of the gate. Shoulders back, head up, but with a slower stride than he was accustomed to seeing, George Reeves sauntered through the gates without looking back.

Once on the other side of the gate, he stood still, looked around, and then saw the black Buick sedan slowly approach and stop in front of him.

"Need a ride?" Benny teased.

George walked up to the car, opened the door, and quickly got inside acting as if expecting someone to come, tap him on the shoulder, and say he wasn't a free man after all. He inhaled and then slowly released a deep breath.

Leaning in, he and Benny gave each other dap. "Man, it feels good. You have no idea."

"Yea, I know. A cop behind bars as a prisoner can be a dangerous thing, huh?"

"Yea, but no more looking over my shoulder, not like that."

Benny drove out of the parking lot and then accelerated once he got out on the public highway.

"Man, it's good to have you out of that place."

"Man, it's good to be out of that dungeon."

"Anywhere you wanna stop before I take you home to your waiting misses?"

"She's waited twenty four months, she can wait another coupla hours. Take me to that spot on Summer. You know the place."

"Yea, they have the best pancakes."

"I've been feening for some of them ever since I got locked up." They drove and chatted up along the way. "Where's my man?"

"Hezekiah?"

"You know it."

"He's gearing up for his trial. Been going back and forth meeting his team of lawyers."

"Hopefully, they'll get him off. It's no fun being behind bars, fed time or not. But he knows about it. It wouldn't be his first time, but no matter, you never get used to having your freedom taken away from you. Somebody telling you when to fart, when to shower, when to eat."

"I haven't been there," Benny said, "and I don't plan on ever going."

"Where's powder head?"

Benny laughed as he made a right turn. "Dee?"

"You know it."

"You know Hezekiah got rid of her. Haven't seen or heard from her in months. She knows what's good for her if she comes back around."

"I know he said he told her to get lost. Then again, she's a hard one to get rid of. I thought she may have weaseled her way back around."

"Nah, I guess she understood Hezekiah wasn't with the crap this time."

"You not serving her anymore?"

Benny shook his head. "No way. When Hezekiah said cut her off, I cut her off."

"Hah, I wonder how she's dealing with that?"

"I don't know and I sure as heck don't care."

"What about my lady. You seen her?"

"Yea, last week. Man, your wife is a real trooper. She's down for you, but I'm not telling you nothing you don't know already."

"Yea she is. Between her, you, and Hezekiah keeping money on my books, I was straight as straight could be up in there. She stayed writing me letters and sending me pictures. Kept me in the loop about what was going on out here."

Benny nodded.

"After I feed my face, I need you to take me to your spot, hook me up with one of your honeys before I go home to the wife. Know what I mean?"

Benny chuckled, "You know it ain't nothing but a word. Man, it's good to have you home."

"Hit up Hezekiah for me."

"Here." Benny passed George a brand new smart phone. "It's already charged."

"This me?"

"Of course it is."

"Thanks, Cuz."

"You know I got to look out for you."

"What's Hezekiah's phone number?"

Benny recited Hezekiah's phone number.

George dialed the number and listened as the phone rang.

"Hello."

"Hey, it's me."

"Yea, I know. Got your number saved into my phone. Welcome home, Georgie boy."

"I'm headed to snap up something to eat and then Benny is going to take me on an adventure to meet one of his honeys before I head to the house."

Hezekiah laughed. "Good for you. I have to meet with my attorneys in a couple of hours. Whaddaya say we meet up out here at my place later tonight or tomorrow."

"Probably tomorrow. I got to spend time with the wife, you know."

"Understood."

"Okay, so we'll talk later."

"Yea...and welcome home, man."

"Thanks."

Hezekiah ended the call.

34

*"Never too old, never too bad, never too late,
never too sick to start from scratch once again."*
Bikram Choudhury

*D*etria's self-made promise to make a change in her life was slowly working for her. She wasn't using as much as she used to, mainly because of Hezekiah cutting her off. It was hard to find another supplier, at least one that she trusted to give her the best of the best. She continued to battle with her addiction but she refused to go into rehab. Hezekiah telling Benny to cut her off was probably a blessing in disguise. However, the withdrawals from the drug, though not as serious as withdrawing from other hard drugs like opioids and heroin, Detria experienced the more psychological withdrawal than anything. Unfortunately, it didn't necessarily make cocaine withdrawal any easier to cope with. Part of the withdrawal symptoms she'd read about online were applicable to her, but she fought hard to deal with getting off the drug.

Depression was probably the hardest. She felt unhappy, had anxiety, was irritable with Priscilla more than usually. Her sleep was uneasy as she was attacked by nightmares and lucid type dreams.

One thing she incorporated into her life was prayer. She kept her promise to Priscilla and attended church with her almost every Sunday, unless she had a tough night dealing with her uneasy sleep patterns.

Priscilla was a lifeline for Detria. Knowing about Detria's addiction, was a good thing for Detria because Priscilla did whatever she could to help her through the tough times of withdrawal.

Another source of support, although she didn't know that her sister was addicted to cocaine, was Brooke. Brooke knew Detria used to smoke weed, and she'd known her to dabble in using other drugs, but never knew that addiction had taken hold of her little sister.

Detria, nonetheless, reached out to Brooke and the two of them rekindled their sibling relationship. Brooke was ecstatic, and so were their parents. Detria hardly ever visited or called her parents or her sister, but all that was changing, and the family was grateful. Her mother was especially happy. Seeing her daughter more was an answered prayer. Now all she needed was for Detria to reach out to Elijah, her seven-year old son.

Elijah was growing up fast and the only mother he truly accepted was his stepmother. It was no fault of his own, and Detria understood that. It wasn't her fault she never wanted children, and after having lost Baby Audrey in that horrific crash, she couldn't see herself being a full-time mother to any child. Elijah, she felt was better off living with his father and his father's wife.

"Brooke, what time will you be here?" Detria asked her sister.

"I should be on my way in about ten minutes. I took these pot pies out of the oven for the boys and John since I won't be here when they get home from the game. All I have to do now is get my bag and keys and I'll be heading out the door."

"Okay, see you soon."

Detria, Brooke, and their mom had a full Saturday planned. It had been years since the three of them spent time together like this. Occasionally, Detria visited her parents and her sister and her family, but those time were few and far between. Detria's life had been blinded by self-sabotage. She allowed the drugs to overtake her. Her need for acceptance since the accident was paramount in her life, causing her to accept being treated less than by not only men but people in general. It was time out for that. No matter how much she cared about Khalil McCoy, she had to keep telling herself the truth—he did not want her. He used her, got her money, her body, and what had she gotten in return? Nothing but heartache. It was the story of her life, from being kicked to the curb by Stiles, Skip, Hezekiah, and most recently Khalil, she was ashamed and embarrassed. Today was a new day and she was going to make the best of it. Hopefully, once she got her life together, things would start working out for her. It surely couldn't get any worse. At least she hoped it couldn't.

The weather was pleasant but on the cooler side so Detria dressed warm in a long sleeve watercolor print tunic, a pair of straight leg jeans and a pair of burgundy knee length riding boots. For the first time in a minute, she was excited for what the day with her sister and mom might bring.

"Looking forward to seeing you when I come back," Stiles texted Victoria while he sat on the plane waiting for takeoff.

He'd seen her twice before leaving for Houston, and boy was he glad he did. Once they met for lunch during her lunch break at work. Last night, he picked her up for dinner and they went to a Mexican restaurant. Again, he couldn't quite define why, but he found her to be easy to talk to and even easier on the eyes. A beautiful, brown-haired, stylish woman, intelligent, with an adventurous side he found titillating. He really liked her and he wanted to get to know more about her.

This might be the perfect friendship. I'm based in Houston; she's in Memphis. She has her own life, career, and the distance would keep us, or me, from taking things too far too fast. This might work after all.

He sent a final text. "About to take off. Have to turn off the phone."

Victoria read the text and smiled. *He's so sweet and thoughtful. I could really like you, Reverend Stiles Graham. I could like you a lot.* "Ok. Hav a safe flight. Call or text later if you want to."

Stiles smiled when he read her reply. *See, that's what I'm talking about. No pressure.* He put his phone on AIRPLANE MODE, rested his head against the headrest, and closed his eyes. It had been a good trip to Memphis.

"Just three more weeks and you should be out of that chair. Isn't that exciting?" Pepper sat curled up on the living room sofa with Xavier watching the History Channel, chumping pizza, drinking sparkling water, and talking in between commercials.

"I can't wait. I'm sick of being cooped up in this apartment."

"Awe, so you don't like being cooped up in this apartment with me?" Pepper made a funny, pouty face and Xavier laughed.

"You know that's not what I meant."

"Yep, I know you can't resist me." She laughed, then straddled him, and kissed him without abandonment. She pulled back and still straddled across his lap. Reaching over to her left, she picked up the remote and pushed the PAUSE button.

"What are you doing?"

"How do you feel about me, Xavier?"

"Huh, what are you talking about? Where is this coming from?"

"How do you feel about me? It's a simple question that requires a simple answer."

Xavier took hold of her shoulders and looked into Pepper's chocolate brown eyes. How *did* he feel about her? Every time that question came across his mind he pushed it aside. He liked Pepper, but she was the first and only heterosexual relationship he'd had in his twenty-one years on earth. What was he to compare their relationship to? Before Pepper, he had no desire to be with a girl. He called himself having a girlfriend when he was about twelve but even then it didn't feel right. Pepper had hit the nail on the head when she told him she believed he had been molested as a kid. He admitted to her she was right. Was that why he was gay? Was that why this relationship he and Pepper were in felt awkward? They were the best of friends. They had many things in common. They understood one another, at least he thought they did so why was she asking him about his feelings? Yes, he was able to perform as a heterosexual man, and she seemed pleased with his performance, but even so, there was something missing for him. He was satisfied but he wasn't satisfied. It didn't make sense. He was confused and he didn't know how to explain it, but how could he get Pepper to see it?

"I'm waiting." Pepper's anxiety level started to rise the longer Xavier remained silent. He was looking at her but the look in his eyes gave her the impression he was looking past her, like his mind was on something, or someone, else.

"I don't know. Look, one thing that makes this work for us is we've always been able to tell each other everything. I've shared things with you I've never shared with anyone."

"So what's different now?"

"I don't know, Pepper. I like you a whole lot. We get along. We like a lot of the same things. Even the sexual part of our relationship is good, but..."

"But what, Xavier? Talk to me."

"It still doesn't feel quite right. It's like I'm pretending to be someone I'm not. You know what I mean? I don't know how else to express it."

Pepper looked back into his eyes and then she kissed him. Not a passionate kiss this time, but a light kiss. "We should get married."

Xavier reared his head back, taken totally off guard with her statement. "What?"

"You said it yourself. We make a good team. We enjoy the same things. We make each other happy. We're good together when it comes to sex. Plus, we like each other. We don't have to be in love. I think love is overrated anyway. And this tug of war you have going on with your sexuality is no different than someone who says they're in love with two people."

"Uh, okay, but how will marriage solve anything? What will it prove?"

"It will prove that we're two young people who have the same goals, dreams, desires, and aspirations. You've said you wanted children one day. We can make children, Xavier. We can make beautiful children—together. Soon or later those feelings you're at war with will dissipate and we'll be even happier than we are now."

Xavier listened. What Pepper was saying made some sense. But whether he was gay or not, was he ready for marriage? For a lifetime commitment with Pepper? If he was with Ian or some other man would he be ready to settle down and have a family at the age of twenty-one?

"If you're thinking about how young we both are, that's a no-brainer because couples our age get married every day, Xavier. And you know I'll support you and be behind you in whatever career you choose. Whether that means remaining at Holy Rock or if you want to move away and go follow your dreams somewhere totally different. I'm a free spirit. I just want us to be together. You're my best friend."

Xavier looked at her again and hugged her tightly. "And you're mine, Pepper. I love you."

Pepper pulled back. This time he saw tears in her eyes and Pepper never cried. "I love you. So what do you say?"

"I say, let's do this."

35

*"We come to love not by finding a perfect person,
but by learning to see an imperfect person
perfectly." Sam Keen*

Eliana and Khalil's relationship was growing stronger every day. Khalil allowed a piece of his heart to be given to Eliana. He was preparing himself for his first lady. He didn't know when it would be, but he planned to ask for her hand in marriage.

"I say if you don't love her, don't do it, man," Omar told him as they stood outside the gym talking after their work out.

"That's it. I've never been in love. I don't know how I'm *supposed* to feel."

"I've been married for five years, bro, and I'll tell anybody Jordyn is the love of my life. I can't see my life without her in it. She's given me kids, a happy home and man the sex is amazing."

Omar and Khalil laughed and fist bumped. "But seriously, not all days are good days. We've had some real knock down drag out fights to the point I had to leave the house to cool off, but I never once thought about divorce. I think she would say the same. So I guess what I'm saying is for us love is more about the two of us liking each other, about us being each other's best friends, and about commitment to one another and our marriage. She's the woman I plan on spending the rest of my days with. If you can't see yourself waking up to Eliana every single day for the rest of your life and being happy about it, you don't need to ask her to marry you. She's not the one, bro."

Khalil looked at his friend. "I have a lot to think about then. I mean, I believe she could be the one. She meets a lot of the criteria you set out. We don't have kids or anything like that and we've only been seeing each other for I guess a little over a year. I can say she makes me not want to cheat on her, although I have, but I'm done with that—I think." He was thinking about Dee and a couple other females he'd smashed, but that was over and done. He'd finally gotten through Dee's head that he wasn't interested in her. He hadn't heard from her and even if she did try to contact him he still had her number blocked. But there was a time a blocked number wouldn't have stopped her because she would have been showing up at Holy Rock insisting on seeing him, or leaving notes on his car. She'd done none of that this time. Boy, was he glad.

"As for the sex between us, it's all that." They laughed and fist bumped again. "But waking up and looking over at the same female for the rest of my life? Man, that's a tough one. I don't know if I can smash just one female forever."

"Then maybe you know the answer already, bro. 'Cause you can't be out there stepping out on your lady, not if you love her. At the end of the day, you know what?"

"What's that?"

"It's a decision you make. A commitment. Either you decide this is who you're going to be with the rest of your life through good times, bad times, ups, downs, whatever sickness, health, just like the vows say or you should stay single until you meet someone who you want to make that commitment with."

"I hear ya. And you're right. I have a lot of thinking to do. So enough of that, I'm going to head to the house. We can hook up later at my house if you want to watch the game. A couple other guys are coming over, Casey, Devon and Roger. We're going to order some food, and push back a few cold ones."

"I'll let you know. I need to see if Jordyn has anything planned first, but more than likely I'll be over."

"Cool." Khalil changed the subject. "My father's trial starts next Wednesday."

"Oh yea. You going?"

"Wouldn't miss it even if my life depended on it. I can't wait to see that fool found guilty. It'll teach him not to mess with me."

"Didn't you say he was there when your li'l bro had the accident? I thought you said he sounded like a changed man."

"That man will never change. Even if he did, he still needs to pay for what he did to my family. You talking about marriage and love being a commitment. Look at him. What kind of commitment did he have for my mother and for his kids?"

"Yea, I know that had to be tough on you and your family. I'm sorry about that, but at least when and if you ever decide to walk down the aisle, you'll know the kind of husband and family man you *don't* want to be."

"Yea, fa sho. Anyway, I'm out. See you at the crib later."

"Yea, see ya." The friends parted ways and walked to their cars.

Fancy accompanied Xavier to his doctor's appointment. The report he received was a good one. Dr. Daniels removed Xavier's cast and ordered outpatient physical therapy so Xavier could regain full mobility or as much mobility as possible.

While Xavier was taken to the other side of Dr. Daniel's medical office to be introduced to the physical therapists, he and Fancy took the opportunity to chat.

The two of them had been in conversation starting a week after they saw each other at Stiles' reception. They didn't talk on a daily basis but they did talk several times a week. Through conversations they learned more about each other. Like Fancy, Micah was a divorcee. He had three children; one adult son, an adult daughter, and a seventeen-year-old son. He resided in a condo on the river in downtown Memphis and was originally from Pennsylvania. He had been in Memphis since his late twenties and was 48 years old.

Fancy opened up to him cautiously, being careful not to come off as a thirsty divorcee. She made it known she was a spiritual woman and especially close to her family and her church.

He hadn't asked her out, but all that changed today.

"Would you like to have lunch after church this Sunday?"

"Yes, sure."

"Our church services end at twelve thirty. We can have a lunch or we can wait until later and have dinner. It's your choice."

"Let's do lunch. Our last Sunday service is over at noon."

"Should I pick you up?"

"Sure. I'd like that. Why don't you pick me up from Holy Rock, if that's not a problem."

"Certainly not. I should be there by one."

"Sounds good."

Micah smiled at Fancy. He didn't date or go out too often because of his busy schedule, but Fancy was a woman he wanted to make time to get to know. Today, he hoped she would come to his office with her son and she had. It presented him with the perfect opportunity to see her again. He had intentions to ask her out before now, but hadn't done so. Most evenings when he got home it was late, he was exhausted, and he had to get right back up at four o'clock the next day to go to the hospital to start his rounds all over again. It was a taxing profession but it was one that he'd dreamed of doing since he was a little boy. His father was a pediatrician and his mother a retired registered nurse. He had a younger sister who had recently completed her residency in Chicago so he came from a line of medical professionals.

He hoped having lunch with Fancy McCoy would be just as entertaining as it was when they talked on the phone. The last time he dated, seriously, was three years ago. Most of the women he dated were nurses, doctors, or women from his church but none had interested him enough to make him want to pursue a serious relationship. Maybe Fancy McCoy would change all that.

36

"You are my greatest adventure." The Incredibles

*"O*MG, we did it!" Pepper kissed and squeezed Xavier around the neck when they stopped at the traffic light. The couple was on their way back to Memphis, having taken a weekend trip to Nashville where they returned as Mr. and Mrs. Xavier McCoy.

As much as Xavier tried to dismiss the memories, he found it almost impossible not to think about the fun time he and Ian had when they made the same trip not long after they first met. What had possessed him to go through with Pepper's crazy idea? *Guess it's no use questioning what I did now. What's done is done. No turning back. God, may this marriage help me put to death the ungodly desires of my flesh for another man.*

"Yea, we did." Xavier managed a forced smile.

"Aren't you happy, babe?"

"Of course. Are you?"

"You know it."

"But we agreed not to tell anyone yet."

"I know, but when we move in together you already know your mother is going to pitch a fit. First, she's going to wanna know why we moved into another apartment and why we're 'living in sin'." Pepper raised her hands in a quote sign.

"We'll tell her in a few weeks. I just want us to have some time to be together, you know as husband and wife."

Pepper kissed Xavier on the cheek, hugging him again and again.

"Pepper, you're going to cause a wreck. Quit it already," Xavier laughed and pulled away.

"I can't help it. I'm just so happy."

"Me too," he faked. "Me too. Hey, my father's trial is coming up in a few days. I'm going to be there. Just want you to know."

"Yes, I know. You told me already. Have the two of you still been communicating?"

"Not a whole lot."

"How do you feel about it? I know when you were discharged from the hospital and found out he had been visiting you and checking on you, you said it meant a lot to you."

"Yea, it did, still does. He's the last person I thought would be concerned about my well-being. It made me realize that maybe he still had some love for his family, for me. He always condemned my life choice. It was like he never listened, never wanted to hear what I had to say, never seemed to respect my choices. I feel like the black sheep of the family. Even my mother never wanted to accept who I am." His countenance changed as he drove. The sadness in his voice was obvious and Pepper listened intently.

Pepper loved Xavier, understood what he was saying, but no matter his feelings about Ian or any other man, she wanted him for herself. Now she had him. She was his wife, and if it took the rest of their lives, she was going to spend it making him love her.

"You sure about this?"

"Nope," Khalil responded as he and Omar walked around the upscale jewelry store.

Omar laughed lightly. "Man, then why are we here?"

"I'd like to see that one," he said to the jeweler, pointing to a Platinum 2.20 carat round cut Halo engagement ring.

Omar almost seized. "Man, you see the price tag on that baby?"

"Yea, and?"

"And you setting out five figures for a woman you're not even sure you want to marry?"

Khalil stopped, looked around at Omar. "If I'm going to do this, I'm going to do it right. You hear me? No since in half-stepping. Plus, I got the cheese so this is like putting a penny in a bucket."

"Suit yourself. It's your life. I'm not saying Eliana doesn't deserve it. The lady is first class all the way and she seems to have your back at all costs. I think she'll be a ride or die for you, and a darn good First Lady. Still, if you aren't ready for the commitment, all I'm saying is don't be persuaded by what other people think. Listen and follow your own heart, K."

"Thanks, Omar." They gave each other dap and Khalil returned to the task at hand.

"I like it," he said to the jeweler. I like it a lot."

"Would you like to purchase this one, sir?"

"Definitely."

37

*"One day your life will flash before your eyes.
Make sure it's worth watching." Unknown*

Hezekiah was able to walk pretty much on his own, except for the use of a cane for whenever he planned on taking extended trips away from home. His speech was back to normal and for the first time in two years he felt like the man he used to be before the stroke debilitated him.

He sat in the doctor's office waiting for his name to be called. It was time for his six month check-up. He hoped to get the thumbs up from the doctor about getting behind the wheel of a car again. That would be the best news yet for Hezekiah.

He didn't know how many more outside doctor's visits he would have, as his trial date was fast approaching. Scrolling through his phone, he received an email notification. He opened the email and read the message. It was a message from the rehabilitation center where Isabella was residing.

It was good news. Isabella was doing remarkably well. The counselor stated in the email she was a star client and believed the young twenty-year old had a bright future ahead. She said Isabella had stated she wanted to continue her treatment after her discharge, slated for two months. They would help her secure a place to live, help her with child care, and get her acclimated to living a life free of drugs.

Hezekiah was glad to read the good news. As he waited he thought about when he first met Isabella. She was just a teenager. Drugs had clouded his mind too but it was still no excuse for him to sleep with a minor. Like Isabella and Detria, he had done his share of drugs, but he was too old to indulge in stupidity and so he had made a decision to stop indulging around the same time he arranged for Isabella to go into rehab. He occasionally smoked a little weed, but he was done with any of the hard addictive stuff. It was time for him to make a change in his life. He was already facing years of time behind bars if he was found guilty. He didn't need to be in prison and withdraw from drugs at the same time.

All in all, he was happy for Isabella. She was a good girl who had been dealt a lousy hand, but now it seemed that things were turning around for her. Of all the wrong he'd done in his life, he needed to feel that he had begun to turn his life around too.

Speaking of turning his life around, he shot Xavier a text. They had been communicating sporadically through text. Hezekiah didn't know who told Xavier about his visits to the hospital, but whoever told him, Hezekiah owed them a thank you. It helped open the door back up for him to have a relationship, though still strained, with his son. He hadn't seen Xavier face to face. Xavier told him he wasn't ready for that. For Hezekiah, communicating with his son was still a positive start.

As for Khalil, Hezekiah resigned himself to the fact he would never get his money back from Khalil. He still had a problem with the fact Khalil stole from him. No matter if he could prove it or not, his gut told him it was Khalil. Khalil was too much like Hezekiah, so it was no doubt the boy took his stash. Hezekiah was by no means a broke man himself. The 100k Khalil stole was part of the embezzlement money but it was not half of what Hezekiah had put away in places unknown by anyone other than himself.

He had his own stash that he could live on for a minute, but he didn't have the money Khalil had. He wouldn't be surprised if Khalil was pushing millionaire status with the way things were flourishing at Holy Rock.

After leaving the doctor's office, he had an appointment with his attorneys. He had a darn good criminal defense team. His hope was that they were so good they could get him off. George had walked out to his freedom while Hezekiah prayed he wouldn't be taking his friend's place behind bars.

The courtroom was partially full. Fancy, Khalil, Stiles, and several of the ministerial staff were present.

"There's that snake, George," Fancy noted to Khalil.

"Yea, I saw him when he first slithered in here. Didn't know he'd gotten out of prison."

"Neither did I," Fancy replied.

"Look, it's your father. He's walking," Fancy looked surprised and whispered to Khalil.

"Yea, good for him," Khalil responded. "He'll need to walk when he's behind bars." Khalil sneered.

Stiles flew in from Houston, anxious to be in support of his brother and his brother's family. It seemed this was the only way he would get the opportunity to see Hezekiah.

When he saw Hezekiah saunter in with a team of high profile attorneys, Stiles smiled. *God is good. He's walking! No more wheelchair. Praise, God.*

He didn't know if his brother was innocent or guilty. That wasn't the reason he was here. The jury would determine that. His purpose was to show his full support by being present and accounted for. He would not take sides. Another reason he was in Memphis was because of Victoria. It had been years, well really since Rena, that he'd felt this way. He looked forward to talking to her, to seeing her when they video chatted, to hear her squeaky childlike voice, and her contagious laughter. Their conversations could be serious or hilarious. She was so versatile. He could be vulnerable with her. He still kept the strings of his heart pulled tight, but he allowed them to loosen just a bit more every time they talked. This evening, after he left court, he and Victoria were going to a music festival in Collierville, Tennessee.

"All rise," the bailiff said, pulling Stiles from his thoughts.

38

"It doesn't matter who hurt you or broke you down, what matters is who made you smile again." KushandWizdom

Stiles and Victoria snacked a little at the festival, bee bopped to the music, and enjoyed their time together. Walking to his car, they held hands.

Victoria could see herself falling in love with him, but she kept her heart at bay, remembering what Fancy told her about Stiles—he was afraid to love. She could identify with him shielding his heart. She was no stranger to heartbreak. Pepper's father had cheated on her with the woman he was married to now, which happened to be a close friend of Victoria's. It hurt something awful and Victoria didn't think she would ever get over it. However, here she was, tonight, having the time of her life with of all people a pastor of a church. She laughed out loud sometimes when she imagined being a First Lady.

On the way home from the festival they stopped to get Chinese takeout.

"Are you sure about going to my place?"

"Yes, the night is young, and I know you aren't going to take a girl home with an empty tummy." They laughed.

"I wouldn't think of doing such a thing."

Arriving at his house, he pulled into the garage, turned off the ignition, opened his door, got out, and went to Victoria's side to open the door for her.

She turned and reached in the back seat for the bag of Chinese food. "Thank you." She stepped out of the car.

"*Niiice,*" she complimented when she walked inside and Stiles gave her a quick tour.

"Thanks. I like it. It's a good neighborhood, quiet, and the house is perfect for me."

They gathered in the kitchen. "You mind?" Victoria inquired as she walked over to the cabinet and began opening drawers.

"Not at all."

Victoria found silverware and brought them to the table. Next, she returned to the cabinets and retrieved two glasses. From there, she opened the stainless steel refrigerator. "Would you like water or what about some of this wine you have in here? Your choice."

"Let's do both."

"Gotcha."

Stiles watched as Victoria easily moved around the space. She seemed so comfortable, like she'd been here a thousand and one times when this was her first time being in his home. Actually, this was the first time since his return to Holy Rock and Memphis that he'd invited any one to his humble abode. First, whenever he did come to Memphis he was always on the move. By the time he finished his ministerial duties he wanted nothing more but to come home and chill. Second, there was nobody, other than maybe Fancy or her sons who he would feel comfortable inviting to his place.

Victoria changed all of that, evident by her prancing around singing one of the songs they'd danced to at the festival.

They ate their Chinese food. Victoria had spring rolls and tofu fried rice no egg while Stiles dined on spring rolls and vegetable linguini.

"This is to die for," Victoria said as she took a forkful of rice into her mouth.

"Yea, every time I come to Memphis, I try to make sure I stop by this place. It's the best I've had."

"I've never stopped there. Then again, it's not too often that I venture on this side of town, unless it's to go shopping. I guess I never paid attention to it."

After eating, Stiles invited her into his den or 'man cave' as he called it. He turned on his playlist, and he and Victoria sat on the couch, talked, and sipped on the white wine.

"I feel so relaxed," she said. "This has been one of the best evenings I've had in a long, long time. Thank you." She looked into Stiles' eyes.

Stiles reciprocated with a smile and took a sip of his wine before setting it down on the table in front of them.

He returned to his position, but not before cautiously reaching out and pulling Victoria in his arms. Without protest, she accepted, no welcomed, his kiss. It was warm, inviting, and stirred emotions inside of her she hadn't given into for a very long time. What they shared felt right and good, making Stiles throw caution to the wind.

39

"May the bridges I burn light the way."
Dylan McKay

*H*ezekiah's trial lasted nine days before it went before the jury for deliberation. The cramped courtroom was almost packed this time with Holy Rock staff members again, only this time it included Eliana, Sista Mavis, and three quarters of the deacon board, the ministerial staff, and ministry leaders—all anxiously waiting to hear the verdict.

On Hezekiah's side sat George, Benny, along with a handful of other people Fancy and Khalil didn't recognize.

Today, Xavier and Pepper showed up at court. Xavier had been present every day of the trial, but this was Pepper's first appearance, more than likely because she didn't have the perks like Victoria to miss days off work.

Fancy was pleasantly surprised to see Stiles appear with Victoria walking in next to him. It was like an award show instead of a trial.

Fancy gave Victoria a wink and a smile of approval. Looking away from Victoria, she spotted Detria parading into the courtroom and taking a seat in the far back on their side.

"What's *she* doing here?"

"Who?" Khalil looked over his shoulder and grimaced when he saw who his mother was talking about.

Detria did a cute little rolling finger wave at him followed by a wicked looking smile.

Khalil scowled then turned back around to face the front of the court. "Who cares? I certainly don't."

"Some people have no morals." Fancy huffed before turning back around. She looked at Hezekiah sitting at the front of the courtroom with his lawyers. As much as she didn't want to admit it, the man looked doggone good. His premium Italian wool suit made him look dignified and charming. He'd grown a close facial beard, something she'd never seen on him. The close to the skin beard was mingled with bits of gray, making him look sophisticated, debonair and oh so fine.

Hezekiah wasn't called to take the stand during the trial, but the day before there had been a huge uproar when the defense attorney accused Fancy, Khalil, and Xavier up setting up their father because he had chosen to leave their mother and divorce her.

This was Stiles' first day in attendance, so he was spared hearing the sometimes horrid accusations that made Hezekiah's family look like spiteful, vengeful and jealous people. This farce had no doubt been fed to the attorneys by Hezekiah. It certainly might cause the jurors doubt of Hezekiah's guilt.

Hezekiah looked over his shoulder. His and Fancy's eyes met. An electric like shock raced through her body. He still had a magnetic effect on her and she hated that about him. After all he'd done to cause upset in her life, she still had feelings for the man.

Hezekiah nodded and gave her one of his charming smiles. *You're one sexy woman, Fancy McCoy. Why did you have to ruin what we had?*

The bailiff appeared. "All rise. The Honorable Judge Meredith Gray presiding."

The judge appeared through a door at the left front side of the courtroom. Climbing the three steps, she took her seat at behind the judge's bench.

"You may be seated," the bailiff instructed and everyone returned to their seats.

"Do we have a verdict?" Judge Gray asked.

"Yes, your honor, we do."

The jury foreman passed the verdict to the bailiff who took it to the judge.

"Mrs. Foreman, members of the jury, have you reached this verdict unanimously?"

"Yes, your honor," the jury members responded.

Opening the sealed envelope and removing the piece of paper, she read it.

"What is your verdict?" the judge asked.

"Your honor," stated the jury foreman, "the jury finds the defendant, Hezekiah McCoy...."

Fancy, Khalil, and Xavier sat in their seats on pins and needles. Detria held her paralyzed hand inside the other and clinched her teeth. George and Benny sat stoic, and Sista Mavis mumbled a short prayer for God's will to be done.

Stiles didn't want to see his brother return to prison, but at the same time, if Hezekiah was guilty he wanted justice to be served.

"We the jury find the defendant, Hezekiah McCoy—NOT GUILTY."

Gasps, thank you Lord, and oh my God, could be heard throughout the courtroom.

Hezekiah clasped his hands together, and immediately looked upward toward the ceiling. "Thank you!"

His lawyers gathered around and embraced him.

Departing the courthouse, Khalil was furious and in a state of utter disbelief. How could they have found his father not guilty? It didn't make sense.

Walking outside and down the steps of the courthouse with his mother, Eliana, Xavier, Pepper, Stiles, and Victoria flanking each side of him, Khalil halted briefly when Hezekiah appeared at the bottom of the steps.

Hezekiah stood, hands clasped, and waited for Khalil and his entourage.

"What do you want?" Khalil swallowed hard, lifted his chin, and boldly met his father's gaze.

"Stop, I want to hear what he has to say." Xavier stepped up almost like he was defending his father.

"I just want to say I forgive you, son." He then looked at Fancy and all who gathered around Khalil. "I forgive you all."

Turning and walking away just as quickly as he'd walked up, George and Benny stood on each side of him and the three of them walked toward Benny's car.

Looking back at his family one more time, he said to George and Benny while shaking his head and laughing wickedly, "Man, those folks at Holy Rock."

The series continues Fall 2019

Words from the Author

$\mathcal{T}$his series keeps revealing so much to me each and every time I write the next installment. Just when I think things are about to change for the good between the McCoy's and the Graham's, life throws another curveball. But isn't that the way it is in REAL LIFE? Just when we think everything is going our way, or things have changed for the better, something can come soaring into our lives and disrupt everything.

Both of these families are interconnected. Both have some serious issues personally and family wise. Sons pitted against fathers. Fathers pitted against sons. Betrayal. Adultery. Backstabbing. Mistrust. Jealousy. Anger. The list can go on and on.

Yet...

The one thing they each have in common is their belief system. They are believers in God. They pray. They repent (*sometimes*). They seek forgiveness (*occasionally*) and like all of us, believers or not, they are imperfect vessels.

However, the good news remains true: We all fall short but we can all be forgiven. We all make mistakes. Yet, God, the Supreme One, loves and accepts us unconditionally—flaws and all.

The McCoys and the Grahams are no different even though they're in a story book!

Contact information
www.sheliaebell.net
www.sheliawritesbooks.com
sheliawritesbooks@yahoo.com
www.facebook.com/sheliawritesbooks
@sheliaebell (Twitter & Instagram)
@literacyrocks (Instagram)

Follow me on Amazon bit.ly/sheliabell

Please join my mailing list for literary updates
and new book release information
www.sheliawritesbooks.com

If you enjoyed this book please go to your favorite
review site and leave a positive review!

Follow my Amazon Author Page bit.ly/sheliabell

Other links to my books

bit.ly/sheliaebell
bit.ly/sheliabn